Ty caught her upper arm,
hauled her up, spun her around
and pressed his mouth to hers.

Madelyn knew if she were ever going to faint
in her life, this would be the minute. His mouth
rubbed solidly against her lips to disarm her, then
parted her lips and absolutely annihilated her.

As quickly as he grabbed her, though, Ty let her
loose and he stepped back. Madelyn gazed up
at him, too startled by the power of his kiss to
breathe, let alone speak.

But Ty didn't seem to have the same problem.
"Watch yourself, Miss Maddy," he warned. "I'm
a man who sees what he wants and takes it. If
you're going to work for me, you either have to
stop flirting with me or accept the consequences."

* * *

Baby Before Business (SR July 2005)
Prince Baby (SR September 2005)
Snowbound Baby (SR November 2005)

Dear Reader,

It's two days before Christmas, and while the streets of New York City are teeming with all the sights and sounds of the holiday, here at Silhouette Romance we're putting the finishing touches on our July schedule. In case you're not familiar with publishing, we need that much lead time to produce the romances you enjoy.

And, of course, I can't help boasting already about the great lineup we've planned for you. Popular author Susan Meier heads the month with *Baby Before Business* (SR #1774), in which an all-work Scrooge gets his priorities in order when he discovers love with his PR executive-turned-nanny. The romance kicks off the author's new baby-themed trilogy, BRYANT BABY BONANZA. Carol Grace continues FAIRY-TALE BRIDES with *Cinderellie!* (SR #1775), in which a millionaire goes in search of the beautiful caterer who's left her slipper behind in his mansion. *A Bride for a Blue-Ribbon Cowboy* (SR #1776) introduces Silhouette Special Edition author Judy Duarte to the line. Part of the new BLOSSOM COUNTY FAIR miniseries, this romance involves a tomboy's transformation to win the cowboy of her dreams. Finally, Holly Jacobs continues her PERRY SQUARE miniseries with *Once Upon a Prince* (SR #1777), featuring the town's beloved redheaded rebel and a royal determined to woo and win her!

And don't miss next month's selection led by reader favorites Judy Christenberry and Patricia Thayer.

Happy reading!

Ann Leslie Tuttle
Associate Senior Editor

Please address questions and book requests to:
Silhouette Reader Service
U.S.: 3010 Walden Ave., P.O. Box 1325, Buffalo, NY 14269
Canadian: P.O. Box 609, Fort Erie, Ont. L2A 5X3

SUSAN MEIER

Baby
Before
Business

Bryant Baby
Bonanza

SILHOUETTE *Romance*®

Published by Silhouette Books

America's Publisher of Contemporary Romance

SILHOUETTE BOOKS

ISBN 0-373-19774-8

BABY BEFORE BUSINESS

This edition published by arrangement with Harlequin Books S.A.

® and TM are trademarks of Harlequin Books S.A., used under license.
Trademarks indicated with ® are registered in the United States Patent
and Trademark Office, the Canadian Trade Marks Office and in other
countries.

Visit Silhouette Books at www.eHarlequin.com

Printed in U.S.A.

SUSAN MEIER

is one of eleven children, and though she has yet to write a book about a big family, many of her books explore the dynamics of "unusual" family situations, such as large work "families," bosses who behave like overprotective fathers, or "sister" bonds created between friends. Because she has more than twenty nieces and nephews, children also are always popping up in her stories. Many of the funny scenes in her books are based on experiences raising her own children or interacting with her nieces and nephews.

She was born and raised in western Pennsylvania and continues to live in Pennsylvania.

THE SWAP

His Turn: Ty's Rules for Madelyn

1. Keep the baby clean and happy.

2. Hire a nanny so you can return to your job as my PR executive.

3. Keep your parents out of my house.

4. Don't think you can change me, even if we've shared a kiss or two!

Her Turn: Madelyn's Rules for Ty

1. Leave work early so you can spend some time with the baby.

2. Donate playground equipment.

3. Start saying hello to your employees!

Note to self: Now that you've seen him outside the office, try to ignore the fact that this all-work Scrooge is _sexy...and truly good at heart!_

Chapter One

"You sent for me?"

Madelyn Gentry entered Ty Bryant's executive office, and when he looked up from the paper he was reading she just barely suppressed a gasp. He was *gorgeous*. Thick black hair perfectly matched his onyx eyes and accented his character-filled, strong-boned face. His impeccable black suit, white shirt and silver tie spoke of elegance and sophistication—the kind of elegance and sophistication she didn't expect to find in a scrooge or ogre, as his employees referred to him.

"Are you the PR *woman* my brother hired?"

"Yes, I'm Madelyn Gentry," she said, ignoring the slight in the way he said "woman" as she extended her hand to shake his, but Ty Bryant acted as if he didn't see the gesture and tossed the paper he'd been reviewing across his desk.

"What's this?"

Madelyn picked up the sheet and glanced at it. "It's the details of your PR event," she said, smiling as she sat on one of his two guest chairs.

But Ty's livid expression caused her smile to fade. He might be one of the most attractive men on the planet, but he could be pretty darned scary-looking. If nothing else, he was intimidating.

Still, that didn't surprise her. His employees had complained about him all three days he had been away from the office for his cousin's funeral. Plus, Ty's brother Seth had filled Madelyn in on Ty's background. She knew the Bryant brothers had lost their parents when Ty was twenty and Ty had taken responsibility for his fifteen- and eighteen-year-old siblings. He had struggled to support them with the family's ailing construction company and, against the odds, had transformed the local contractor into a supersuccessful development business.

It was a no-brainer to realize Ty's difficult life had made him somewhat harsh. But, justifiably grouchy or not, the guy had to clean up his act. That was why his much nicer brother Seth had hired her.

"You need to get out into the community—"

"Cancel it."

Madelyn took a silent breath, remembering how Ty's employees had called him Tyrant Ty, the boss from hell. As far as Madelyn was concerned, if his employees couldn't even be kind to him while he was away for a funeral, there was no telling what they would say to the *Wall Street Journal* reporter scheduled to arrive in three weeks. Madelyn couldn't let a member of the media anywhere near the unhappy residents of Porter, Arkansas, until Ty's employees at least stopped name-calling.

"I can't. It's all arranged. Besides, you—"

"I said cancel it. I will give the *Wall Street Journal* an interview because Seth thinks it's necessary to get our company name in a newspaper with national circulation so we're recognized when we begin bidding on federal projects. But I won't participate in a sap fest."

Madelyn gasped. "This isn't a sap fest! You're presenting playground equipment to a day care! You need this event to soften your reputation in the community."

That made him laugh. "Ms. Gentry, I spent fifteen years getting this reputation, there's no way in hell I want it softened."

So, he was an ogre by choice. Great. There was no way she could repair his image. The best she could hope for was that his employees would feel better about him after he gave the gym sets to the day care, and pray the afterglow from his donation lingered at least until the reporter came to Porter.

"I understand that, but…"

"And I'm not giving away thirty thousand dollars."

"You're not *giving away* thirty thousand dollars. You're donating equipment to the day care that babysits most of your employees' children. Think of it as thirty thousand dollars of goodwill."

"Baloney. Swings and gym sets and volleyballs—"

"Will win over parents," she interrupted, finding the perfect opening to get her point across, but Ty didn't let her finish.

"And that's another thing," he said, rising and tossing a second piece of paper at her. "Who wrote this speech? It's the most disgusting piece of drivel I've ever read. Giving some kid a swing does not turn him into a leader."

"It's not the swing. It's the sense of community…"

"Elitist liberal crap," Ty said, walking to the wall of window behind his desk and looking out at the rural Arkansas town that housed his company. Tall and broad-shouldered, he stood ramrod straight. His dark hair gleamed in the late-afternoon sun. Madelyn couldn't help noticing again that the man was hot, but it was too bad all those good looks were wasted on a grouch.

"The last thing kids need is to be mollycoddled. What they really should learn is to earn what they get and to pull their own weight. If you think otherwise, you're certainly not the person to be doing Bryant Development's public relations. You're fired."

Madelyn blinked, stunned. "What?"

He faced her. His dark eyes were cold and serious. "You…are…fired," he said, enunciating each word as if he were speaking to a slow-witted child. "Pack your things and go."

Madelyn's mouth fell open in complete shock. Suddenly grouch, ogre, scrooge and troll seemed too kind to describe Ty Bryant. Even tyrannical dictator didn't hit the mark. He was the coldest man she had ever met. He was, quite simply, a public relations nightmare and she realized *nobody* was going to clean up this guy's image—not even somebody who desperately needed to.

She was at the end of the money she'd saved while working for a high-powered PR firm in Atlanta. Her father had recovered from the heart attack that had brought her home the year before, but she still didn't feel right about leaving. She and her sister and their two brothers had all moved to other parts of the country to find work, and her parents were alone. Arlene sold medical supplies in the northwest and couldn't live in Arkansas. Jeff and Marty both worked for big corporations that didn't have offices anywhere near Porter. Madelyn was the logical choice to return to their hometown.

She'd tried drumming up consulting jobs, but in little Porter she didn't get much work. She wrote a few press releases for local politicians and helped some people enhance their résumés, but that had been about it.

Seth Bryant had dangled two enticing possibilities when he offered her this assignment. First, working for Bryant Development would give her exposure enough to get new clients—maybe not in Porter but close enough that she could still live in Porter. And second, Seth planned to talk Ty into creating a permanent PR department. If she succeeded in cleaning up Ty's image, she would be the logical choice to head it.

But after meeting Ty Bryant she had to be realistic. He wasn't the kind of guy positive PR could change overnight—or even in the three weeks she had before the reporter arrived—and there was a bigger chance she would fail than succeed. Then there would be no job at Bryant Development. Plus, if word leaked that she'd failed, she wouldn't attract new individual assignments. She might even lose the résumé business she had. Either way, she would be returning to Atlanta.

"Excuse me?" Joni O'Brien, Ty's secretary, poked her head into Ty's office doorway, and Madelyn and Ty's attention turned to the petite brunette.

Clearly annoyed, Ty said, "Joni, I'm meeting with someone. You know better than to disturb me."

"Well, okay. Then I won't tell you that I'm leaving to take my kids to the dentist or that the attorney for your cousin Scotty's estate is here to see you."

"Why is Scotty's attorney here?" Ty asked, obviously surprised by the visit.

"I think I'd better let him answer that." Joni turned toward the reception area and said, "Mr. Hauser, why don't you go ahead in?"

"Joni! I can't see him…" Ty began, going from annoyed to furious in under five seconds, but when Pete Hauser, one of only two attorneys who had offices in Porter, stepped into the doorway, Ty stopped talking.

Madelyn's face scrunched in confusion. Pete held two diaper bags and a car seat. His secretary, Renee Brown, stood beside him, holding a little girl Madelyn guessed was about six months old. Wearing a pretty pink dress, white ruffle tights and black buckle shoes, the baby was adorable.

"Sorry about this," Pete said as he and Renee entered Ty's office. "But as you can see, we're really not in a position to wait."

Ty Bryant cast a quick glance at Madelyn Gentry. Medium height and thin, with no-nonsense straight red hair that fell to her shoulders, she didn't look like the perky Pollyanna his brother had described. Though she was only twenty-five, in her green skirt and simple beige top she looked professional and businesslike. But that didn't change the fact that her job was fluff. *Unnecessary* fluff. More akin to *Gossip Grid* and *Night Life* magazines than actual work. Though Ty really didn't know why Pete and his assistant Renee had brought Scotty's daughter to his office, he didn't want anything personal witnessed by a recently fired woman with contacts at all the newspapers on the eastern half of the United States.

After nodding an acknowledgment to Pete, Ty faced Madelyn. "Ms. Gentry, I think our discussion is over, but you look like you want to argue. You're not going to change my mind, but if you still wish to duke it out, you can wait in my secretary's office until I'm finished with Mr. Hauser."

Ty watched Madelyn glance from the baby to Pete and then back to him again. Her bright green eyes displayed confusion. She licked her full, perfect lips as she assessed the situation, but she didn't say a word. She simply rose and left the room.

Ty walked to his office door and closed it. "What's up?" he asked, striding back to his desk.

Pete dropped the two heavy-looking diaper bags onto a convenient chair. "We found Scotty's will today, Ty, and he names you as Sabrina's guardian."

Ty shook his head. "Sorry. Can't do it."

"I don't think you heard me," Pete said. "Scotty's will names you as guardian. It's my responsibility to give you the baby, that's it."

"Oh, come on, Pete, you can't just barge into my office and drop off a child!"

"Yes, I can. As administrator of an estate I do what the will says and the will says you get the baby."

Ty gaped at him. "You're kidding!"

"No." Pete paused, then added, "I assumed Scotty and Misty had spoken with you about this."

"They hadn't." Ty glanced at the little girl in Renee's arms. With her curly blond hair, pink dress and tiny black shoes, Sabrina looked like an angel, but Ty knew better. Kids were work, but Sabrina was a *baby*. There were *years* of trouble in this kid's future. He wouldn't start with high school as he had with Seth or even college as he had with Cooper. He would start with bottles and diapers and sandboxes and preschool, and build up to cars and proms.

No way he was doing this.

"Here, take her," Renee suggested with a smile, offering the baby to Ty.

Eyes wide with horror, Ty stepped back.

"Oh, come on," Renee cajoled. "She's a sweetie. You'll be fine," she insisted, forcing Sabrina into Ty's arms.

He had no choice but to catch the baby as Renee let go. He awkwardly juggled Sabrina into the crook of his elbow, then peered down at her as she raised her gaze to meet his. For ten seconds, she looked at him as he studied her. Then, without a sniff of warning, her lips puckered, her eyes filled with tears and she issued a blistering wail that would have singed off his hair if she had been closer.

"What about Misty's parents?" Ty asked, shifting her over his shoulder and patting her back in a clumsy attempt to quiet her while he stalled Pete long enough to find a way out of this.

"Scotty and Misty's wills both give you custody, but even if they didn't Misty's dad is in remission from cancer," Pete shouted because Ty's back-patting wasn't calming Sabrina down. If anything, her crying seemed to get louder. "Given the state of his health, Misty's parents didn't think they were capable of dealing with a baby. They were relieved this afternoon when we read the wills and saw you got custody."

That information poured over Ty like cement, freezing him in place and numbing his brain. Because Scotty's parents had been killed in the same accident that took Ty's parents, and both Misty and Scotty were only children, Misty's parents were Ty's only hope. There wasn't going to be a way out of this. Sabrina screamed all the louder.

Pete pointed to the first of two diaper bags he had deposited on the chair in front of Ty's desk and yelled, "Bottles are in there."

Ty cast a baffled look at the brightly printed container and shouted, "Bottles?"

Renee removed the diaper bag hanging on her shoulder and set it beside the other two. "And this one is full of disposable diapers," she said, also loud enough to be heard over Sabrina's crying.

"Shhh, shhh, shhh," Ty crooned, panic churning in his stomach. He could not raise a baby! Hell, he couldn't even get her to stop crying! "This isn't going to work, Pete!"

Pete grimaced and raised his voice another notch because Sabrina had somehow gotten louder. "Ty, I'm sorry, but that's not my problem. *You're* named guardian. I gave you the baby. That's the end of my responsibility. What you do now is between you and her grandparents or you and child services."

Child services!

Before Ty had a chance to take that thought any further, his office door burst open and Madelyn Gentry stormed in. She sighed heavily and marched over to Ty. "Really, you guys. What's going on?" she asked as she took the baby from Ty's arms. Without waiting for an answer, she strode to the diaper bags and began rummaging around. "Even through the closed door I could hear this poor child screaming. Were you beating her in here?"

Not at all happy to have a PR guru in the room to witness this disaster, Ty watched Madelyn retrieve a bottle. He knew very well that once she told the story of a lawyer bringing Ty a baby, everyone would assume Sabrina was his illegitimate child. He normally didn't care about rumors, but he also wasn't so stupid as to let one start three weeks before a reporter from the *Wall Street Journal* arrived. Particularly since he could so easily stop it.

"My cousin and his wife died. I got custody of their baby."

"Just like this?" As Sabrina continued screaming, Madelyn arranged her across her arm to feed her and faced Pete. "Without a word of warning, you're dumping this poor baby in his lap?"

"I'm perfectly capable of hiring a nanny," Ty shouted, doing the further damage control of nipping any potential tale of his incompetence in the bud, but his voice echoed around him because Sabrina had stopped crying. Madelyn was leaning against his desk, feeding a bottle to the little girl, who gulped greedily as if she were starving.

Pete laughed and turned to Ty. "You'll be fine," he said, shaking Ty's hand as if to finalize the deal. "Nice seeing you!" he said, as he and Renee hurried out of Ty's office.

Ty glanced at the fired public relations gal. Even though he didn't want to be wowed by her ability to get the baby to quiet down, he had to admit he was. But he was more impressed that she'd come in to help after he'd fired her. Of course, she could have been looking for leverage to get her job back. Ty almost slapped his forehead at his stupidity. Of course, she only came in to get her job back.

He took the suckling baby from Madelyn's arms, careful not to knock the bottle from the infant's mouth. "I believe I just fired you."

Madelyn glanced at the baby and then back at him. Her pretty green eyes were full of confusion, but also concern. "*You're* going to care for this child by yourself?"

"Like I said. I'm perfectly capable of hiring a nanny."

Madelyn studied him for a few seconds and the curiosity left her expression. Her demeanor became professional and she pushed away from his desk. "Yes, you are. I'm sure you'll be fine."

"Of course I'll be fine!" Ty snapped. The fact that she felt entitled to an opinion really rubbed Ty the wrong way. *This* was why he kept his private life private. He didn't like answering to anybody.

Before Ty could say anything further, Madelyn Gentry began striding to the door. Almost simultaneously, Sabrina peered up at him and stiffened in his arms. Ty felt the storm brewing even before the baby spit the bottle out of her mouth and screamed.

He panicked. He might be able to hire a nanny eventually, but he didn't have one now and the only help within a hundred yards was walking out the door.

"Wait!"

Madelyn laughed. "No. You don't want *me* here. Call a relative or a girlfriend."

"Shhh-shhh-shhh," Ty whispered, patting Sabrina's back as he inexpertly cuddled her to him. Apparently unimpressed that he let her slobber on his thousand-dollar suit, Sabrina cried all the louder. "With Scotty gone, my brothers are the only blood relatives I have aside from this baby." Sadness rippled through him at the realization that his only cousin was now gone, but he didn't let that show on his face or in his voice as he continued. "And you heard my secretary say she was leaving for the day. She's not even going home. She's taking her kids to the dentist. I couldn't find her if I wanted to."

Madelyn stopped walking and faced him. "No girlfriend?"

He wanted to tell her that was none of her business, but with Sabrina screaming on his shoulder, he only shook his head.

Madelyn sighed, then strode over to Ty. "I should have known no woman would have you." She took the sobbing baby and bottle from Ty.

"I'm single by choice."

"Whatever."

Madelyn arranged Sabrina across her arm, slid the bottle into her mouth again, and resumed her position of leaning against Ty's desk. "Poor baby," she murmured, soothing the child, but irritating the hell out of Ty.

"Poor baby? This kid will have her own personal nanny, whose full-time job will be to cater to her every wish and whim."

"Maybe. But you don't have a nanny now and Sabrina is stuck with *you* tonight."

Ty scowled. Damn it! She was right. A competent nanny couldn't be brought in on a moment's notice, not without investigating his or her background. Which meant he was going to be alone with this baby tonight. And he didn't have a clue of how to keep Sabrina from crying, let alone how to care for her.

But Madelyn Gentry really seemed to know what she was doing.

"So what makes you such an expert about kids?"

"I have three brothers and sisters and eight nieces and nephews," Madelyn said, aware that her ex-boss was up to something because his voice had shifted from rude to curious. "I've fed a bottle or two in my day."

"Yeah, well, I raised two brothers, but Cooper was eighteen and Seth was fifteen when I took over. Until just now, I'd never even held a baby." He paused and glanced at Madelyn. Sounding uncharacteristically vulnerable, he said, "I don't think they like me."

Madelyn couldn't argue that. She knew firsthand that most adults didn't like him. Why should a baby be any different? Still, she didn't trust the sudden spurt of honesty. His vulnerable act could very well be a trick to get her sympathy. She cautiously said, "I take it you haven't had much contact with this child before."

"No. And even if Seth wasn't out of town for the weekend, he wouldn't be any better with her than I am. He's only cooed at her when Scotty brought her to visit."

"Great."

Ty drew a quick breath. "Do you think it's going to be hard to find a nanny?"

Oh, so *that* was it. He was making himself look vulnerable because he needed assistance finding a nanny. Well, sorry. He was out of luck.

"I don't know. I lived in Atlanta for two of the past three years. Any contacts I made there are too far away." Madelyn snuggled the baby closer and Sabrina's sucking slowed, an indication that she was drifting off to sleep. "So I'm afraid I'm not much help."

"Actually, you look like lots of help."

Their eyes met and Madelyn read Ty Bryant's intentions as clearly as if he had spoken the words. He didn't want assistance finding a nanny. He wanted *her* to be the nanny!

Though careful not to jar the baby, she bounced away from his desk. "Oh, no. No. No. No. I am *not* a nanny."

"You might not be a nanny, but you're certainly better with a baby than I am. And Seth's already investigated you. Nobody gets the kind of authorization you got to interview staff and look at our five-year plan unless Seth has human resources run background checks. So you're cleared."

"No."

"I'm not asking you to take the job permanently," Ty angrily retorted as if she were the one being unreasonable. "I only need you for a few days, maybe a week. Just until I have time to properly interview and investigate a few candidates."

"It will take more than a week to interview and investigate candidates!" Madelyn gaped at him. "Do you know what you're asking?"

"Yes."

"No, you don't!" Madelyn emphatically disagreed as she leaned against the desk again to finish feeding Sabrina. "Babies get up in the middle of the night! I'd have to stay at your house!"

"I'd pay you well...."

"It's not a question of money!"

"Okay, then. How about this? I won't simply rehire you to do the PR job, I'll do absolutely everything you want me to do to prepare for the *Wall Street Journal* interview."

That stopped her. And she knew he'd done it on purpose. A sharp negotiator, he'd let her get out all of her objections before he went in for the kill and offered the only things she wanted. The job and his cooperation. "Are you kidding me?"

"No. Do this favor for me and I will do whatever you feel needs doing to make myself look nicer to the reporter," he said, back to sounding like the in-control executive who had fired her, and Madelyn's business instincts shot to red alert. Sure, he made it appear that they were on even terms, but this was the kind of guy who always kept the upper hand. There was a catch here somewhere.

So handsome he could have posed for *GQ*, Ty Bryant strolled closer and didn't stop until he was mere inches in front of Madelyn and Sabrina. "Can I take her?"

Madelyn nodded and eased the nearly sleeping baby into his arms. He nestled the little girl against his chest as she sleepily suckled her bottle, but he didn't move away from Madelyn.

Holding her gaze with his hypnotic brown eyes, he said, "I have something you want. A job. You have something I want. The ability to care for a baby. I'm offering you a simple deal. Take it or leave it."

Feeling mesmerized by his magnetic gaze, Madelyn blinked, but it didn't help. His nearness had caused her heart rate to triple. Her breathing had become feathery and light. She desperately wanted to swallow, but couldn't because she knew he would see and take it as a sign of weakness.

Forcing herself to think his proposition through, she tried to come up with a downside and knew there wasn't one. He might believe he could bully her out of his agreement once he had her commitment, but that wasn't true. His inability to care for Sabrina gave Madelyn a weapon that she wouldn't hesitate to use. Until he hired a nanny, any time he refused to do anything she asked, she would simply leave him alone with the child that he clearly couldn't care for. Then he would either adhere to the terms of their deal, or be miserable. Of course, once he hired a nanny that leverage would be gone, but by then her advance work for the *Wall Street Journal* reporter would be done.

She still didn't trust him.

"Even give away thirty thousand dollars worth of playground equipment and deliver a sappy speech?"

He grimaced but said, "If you honest to God think I need to do that, I will do it."

For all practical intents and purposes, she had a deal. But she couldn't force her mouth to form the words of acceptance. She'd seen his real temperament and demeanor when he fired her. She also remembered all the complaints his employees had made about him. There was a lot of damage to be repaired here. Though confident in her own abilities, she recognized that unless she could figure out a very solid way to get Ty

Bryant to look, sound and behave like a totally different guy before the *Wall Street Journal* reporter arrived, she was going to fail. Because, the truth was, he could do every darned thing she said and still come across as an ogre.

Or, more realistically, Madelyn thought, he would come across as a powerful, distanced executive so wealthy and clueless about the real world he was heartless.

And if an employee got *that* opinion into the *Wall Street Journal* article, it would be all over.

The bottle slipped out of Sabrina's mouth, a sign that she was asleep and Ty set it on the desk, passing within a millimeter of Madelyn's shoulder as he did so.

Madelyn suppressed a shiver, as the room grew unbearably hot. *What the hell was happening to her?*

"Excuse me, Mr. Bryant?"

At the sound of Neil Ringler's voice, Madelyn and Ty looked at the mailroom employee, who was at Ty's door.

"What is it, Neil?" he asked quietly, obviously not wanting to awaken the sleeping baby.

"I'm sorry, but Joni's not here." Neil very cautiously stepped in the room, virtually shaking in his shoes. "And you got this package from a special courier. I...I was just about to leave when it arrived. But I stayed..." He gulped. "You know, so you'd get it. But I can't sign for it. I'm not on that level yet."

"Let Ms. Gentry sign for it."

Again, Ty's voice was quiet and the previously shaking mailroom employee not only gave Ty a baffled look, he also relaxed a bit.

"Here," Neil said, handing the fat envelope to Madelyn along with the delivery log to be signed. As Madelyn put her signature on the appropriate line, Neil faced Ty. "Whose baby?" he whispered.

Ty said, "Shhh!" indicating Neil should lower his voice even more, then very quietly added, "Mine. Sabrina was the daughter of my cousin who was killed. I got custody today and I don't want her to wake up, so grab that log and leave."

Even though Ty's command was straightforward, with his voice softened, it didn't come across harshly, and Neil grinned.

"Okay," he stage-whispered, then snatched the clipboard and left the room.

Madelyn stared at Ty.

"Did you see what you just did?"

Ty faced her. "Don't lecture me on yelling at my employees."

"You didn't yell. You..." She stopped her explanation because if she came right out and told Ty that the soft voice he used while holding the baby made his demand more palatable, he would tell her that was liberal elitist crap. But his quiet tone *had* changed the entire dynamic of his exchange with Neil.

She took a quick breath as an idea began to form. She couldn't have Ty hold a baby until all his employees saw what Neil saw. But as Ty cared for Sabrina over the next few weeks while he looked for a nanny, she probably could teach him to speak more softly. She might even be able to get him to laugh once or twice. Time alone with him and a baby had endless possibilities for inching him toward lightening up.

And any changes Ty made wouldn't be questioned.

Neil would quickly spread the news that Ty had taken in his deceased cousin's baby, and before long every employee in the building would ascribe kindness to their scrooge boss, which they hadn't before. More than that, though, they would ultimately believe that the baby was responsible for any change in Ty's behavior, not the upcoming article.

It was perfect.

"I'll do it."

Ty glanced over and whispered, "What?"

"I'll help you with the baby on the condition that you really do every darned thing I say both with her and for your PR."

Ty smiled victoriously, but Madelyn sternly said, "I mean it. You have to really promise to do what I say. The first time you tell me no, I leave. And you'll be alone with this baby."

"Deal," Ty said, then extended his free hand to shake hers.

Madelyn grasped it and a lightning bolt shot through her and warning bells went off in her head. She had just agreed to spend at least a week or more living with a guy she not only admitted to herself was gorgeous, but with whom she was having all kinds of weird physical reactions.

She stopped that thought because it was ridiculous. The man was a mean-spirited dictator and she was a smart professional woman. Smart women didn't get involved with grouchy self-absorbed men.

"Deal," she said, shaking once as she caught his gaze.

Big mistake. When she met his sexy dark eyes, the zing of attraction exploded through her again. Desperate to distract herself, she glanced at the baby he held, but when she did, she realized what was happening and she almost laughed.

All along she'd noticed Ty was gorgeous, but she hadn't felt an attraction to him until he picked up the baby. The same thing that would ultimately make him attractive to his employees was making him attractive to *her* now: the baby.

Reaching to pull Sabrina from his arms, she said, "Let me take her."

"No, I'm fine with her," Ty argued.

But Madelyn shook her head. "Until we both adjust to this situation, *I'm* holding the baby when we're alone."

Chapter Two

Madelyn carried Sabrina, and Ty lugged her car seat and diaper bags to his black SUV, which was parked beside the private entrance to the Bryant Building—the entrance that prevented him from having to go through the lobby and interact with a boatload of employees on his way to his office in the morning.

After storing the diaper bags in the rear compartment, he tried to install the car seat. But when he couldn't immediately get all the buckles and snaps aligned, he stepped out of the way, took the baby from Madelyn and let her connect it.

He wasn't going to be an idiot about this. Raising Sabrina might be a high priority, but doing menial tasks involved in her upbringing weren't. That was why he had hired the woman beside him.

With the seat installed and the baby contentedly cooing as she pounded on the padded seat guard in front of her, Ty drove Madelyn to her parents' home to retrieve the clothes and accessories she would need for the weekend.

He stole a peek at the woman he'd coerced into helping him. Her straight red hair glistened in the late-afternoon sun. Her smooth pink skin gave her the look of a fresh-faced, all-American girl. For the first time, something very important struck Ty. Madelyn was young. He'd already guessed her age at around twenty-five. At most she had three years of experience in her chosen field. Yet, he'd agreed to let her splash his name all through the papers and get him out in the community for a love fest with people who should already be kissing his behind for providing them with jobs. That side of the agreement wasn't exactly a good deal for him.

The other end of the bargain wasn't a total prize either. He might be getting care for Sabrina, but a stranger—no, an *employee,* someone who could take bits of his personal life into the office—would be living in his home.

Man, he hadn't really thought this through.

They parked on the street in front of the huge Victorian-style house where Madelyn's parents lived. White vinyl siding and modern green shutters had replaced the original exterior treatment of the dwelling that he suspected was built in the 1940s. But the actual shape of the structure hadn't been altered so it managed to retain all of its charm. Flower gardens encircled the front porch. The manicured lawn spoke of a great deal of tender loving care.

If nothing else, Madelyn and her family were neat. Point one in her favor.

Madelyn opened the SUV door and jumped out. "I'll be right back."

Ty had assumed he would wait in the car with Sabrina while Madelyn got her things. But when a series of short bursts erupted from the baby as if she couldn't decide whether or not to cry because Madelyn was gone, Ty punched open his door and leaped out of the SUV. With a potential storm in Sabrina's whimpers of discontent, he didn't have to debate his next move. He quickly pulled the baby out of the little plaid car seat, then scurried to catch Madelyn on the sidewalk.

She stopped and gave him a look he couldn't quite interpret. "Why don't you and the baby wait for me in the car?"

"No way. You're not leaving me with two feet of person that cries when it wants something and can't control its bladder."

Madelyn rolled her eyes and turned away from him, heading to the porch again. "You're going to make a terrific dad."

"Actually, I did make a pretty good dad for my brothers. I think that's why Scotty chose me as the one to be guardian—"

Ty quit talking when he realized he was on the verge of telling a woman he hardly knew some incredibly personal information about himself. But before Madelyn could demand he continue, a sixtysomething man rounded the corner of the house. His crew cut was gray. So was the five o'clock shadow on his chin and jaw. He was also short. But beneath his T-shirt were broad shoulders and a flat stomach.

"W...ho's that?"

"My dad."

Dad?

Oh great! Ty had been on his own for so long he forgot other people had parents. And this guy was a piece of work. He looked like a marine who hadn't yet gotten the message that he was retired. Someone who, if provoked, didn't yell or scream or argue, he punched.

Ty realized another bad thing about his arrangement with his PR gal. Porter's most successful businessman, avowed bachelor and reputed scrooge, had coerced this G.I. dad's obviously young, probably innocent—if only in her father's eyes—daughter into living with him. For money.

Great.

"Hey, little Miss Maddy! Who have you got there?"

Ty stole a peek at the reddening face of his temporary nanny. Not only was her dad not going to like their arrangement, but also Ty was just about certain little Miss Maddy probably already knew that. "Little Miss Maddy?"

"Just shut up." Madelyn mumbled to Ty before she faced her dad. "Ty, this is my dad, Ron Gentry. Dad, this is Ty Bryant."

"I know who Mr. Bryant is. Everybody in town knows Mr. Bryant." He walked over and extended his hand. "The question is, why is he here?"

Oh, just here to get some things for your daughter so she can live with me for a while.

Silencing the voice in his head as he balanced Sabrina on one arm, Ty shook hands with Ron Gentry. "It's nice to meet you."

"Nice to meet you, too." Miss Maddy's dad eyed Ty

speculatively. "You here for dinner? Because Maddy's mom had some big church thing this afternoon. Supper's not going to be for a while."

Before Ty could answer, Madelyn did. "That's okay, Dad. We're not here for dinner. Ty just got custody of this baby—"

"Cute little thing," her dad interrupted, glancing at Sabrina, but his gaze quickly jumped back to Ty because he was definitely more interested in Ty than the baby.

Once again Madelyn came to the rescue. "Yes, she is cute. Her name's Sabrina. But Ty doesn't have a nanny, so I'm going to help him care for the baby this weekend."

Score another point for Miss Maddy. She wasn't one to let anybody intimidate her. Not even her dad.

Liking her direct approach, Ty met Ron's gaze, as Ron said, "All weekend?"

"Maybe longer," Madelyn said, while Ty continued to hold Ron's gaze, taking his cue from Madelyn to face this head-on. "I've helped with Arlene and Jeff's kids. I can certainly care for one baby."

Good one! Ty broke his stare-down with Ron to bestow a look of respect on the big guy's daughter. She had deliberately misinterpreted her dad's concern to steer him off track. Point three. And confirmation that Ty hadn't misjudged her. She could handle this. She could probably handle his PR, too. Even though just thinking about having to go out in public and make nice with a bunch of people who hated him made Ty want to sigh with disgust, at least he knew Madelyn could do the job.

Ron sounded like he was growling when he said, "I wasn't talking about the baby. I was—"

Worried about his daughter sleeping with the town

tyrant, Ty thought, just barely holding back a grimace. But Madelyn didn't let her dad go there.

"You know what, Dad? We'll discuss this later. Right now, I've got to get some things from my room."

With that she turned and jogged up the steps to the porch. Ty took one look at her dad and decided he wasn't hanging around. Explaining this situation was Madelyn's job. And he did mean *job.* He had hired her to work for him, not…not…

An odd feeling tightened his chest when he tried to think of Madelyn and himself together, and he couldn't form the words or the images in his mind. Madelyn was younger than he was. Way too young for him to even entertain a casual fling. She was as safe with him as Sabrina was.

Madelyn didn't feel a qualm of conscience about leaving Ty with her dad. Though she'd staved off her father's questions long enough that she would have time to gather her things, Ty should have been the one doing the talking. After all, this was his plan. Let him justify it to her dad.

But when she turned to grab a few T-shirts from a drawer, Ty Bryant was right behind her. She gasped and clutched her chest. "What!"

"Your dad thinks we're going to sleep together tonight."

She sighed. "Don't worry. If I tell him we won't, he'll believe me."

"You're not my type," Ty continued as if she hadn't spoken. "Too young." She saw him look around at the wedding ring quilt on her bed, her white Priscilla tie-back curtains. "And too nice."

"What? You only date nasty women?"

"Sophisticates," Ty corrected.

Madelyn tossed two pair of shorts in her duffel bag. Right. She knew that. Just as she knew it was wrong to be attracted to him because holding a baby did not change a man's personality, she also knew that the CEO of Bryant Development would have absolutely no interest in her. But that was okay. She didn't want him to be interested in her.

So why the hell did having him in her bedroom make her pulse jump?

Three reasons immediately popped into Madelyn's head. First, with his shiny black hair and obsidian eyes, the man was absolutely delicious-looking. Second, holding the baby softened the hard edge of his personality. And, third, he was two feet away from her underwear drawer. All he had to do was look down to see her collection of lacy panties. Any one of those accounted for why her pulse was jumping. But the third was the best bet.

"Do you want to wait for me in the car?"

"No. I'm fine," Ty assured her as if his comfort were the only thing to be considered.

"*I'm not.* I have to get a toothbrush, underwear and girlie things most guys don't want to see." She drew a long-suffering breath. "Could you just leave?"

For a second it appeared that he would tell her it didn't bother him to see her undies. Not because he wanted a peek at her panties, but because he was trying to prove that sophistication of his. Luckily, he thought the better of it.

He glanced at Sabrina who was happily occupied with a rattle toy, and apparently decided it was safe to be alone with her for a few minutes. "I'll see you in the car."

"Wonderful," Madelyn said, not meaning one syllable of the word.

She packed quickly, and scurried down the steps, but when she rounded the corner to rush to the front door she ran into her mom. A flour-covered apron covered Penney Gentry's cropped jeans and T-shirt. A streak of flour decorated her graying brown hair.

Yet another great. Her dad thought she was moving in with the man who controlled the town and he wasn't happy. But he wasn't a match with Madelyn in a battle of wits because there were certain things he wouldn't talk about in mixed company. Sex being the big one. Which meant he had called her mom home from baking pies for the upcoming church social to talk some sense into his daughter.

Another magic moment in the scrapbook of her life.

"You're spending the weekend with a man?"

"In Atlanta, I could have spent hundreds of weekends with men and you wouldn't have had a clue. But you knew I didn't because you trusted me. Don't spaz on me now, Mom."

"I trusted you because we taught you better."

"So, if you trusted me not to lie to you about Atlanta, that's got to mean I'm not lying now. I really am spending the weekend with Ty Bryant to help him with his baby."

Her mother smiled, making her green eyes twinkle. "You're bad."

"No, I'm good. And if it makes you feel any better, Mr. Bryant assured me he's not interested. I'm too nice for him."

Preoccupied with brushing the flour out of her hair, Penney absently said, "He only dates nasty women?"

"I asked him the very same question." She kissed her

mom's cheek. "Go back to church and finish the pies. I'll be home Monday or Tuesday night. I promised I would stay until he found a nanny, but I figured out in the car on the way over that he can probably hire some-one from a reputable agency temporarily. We may not be able to get someone over a weekend, but Monday or Tuesday isn't unrealistic. As soon as we get to his house I'll have him call a service."

"Okay," her mom said with a smile. "I'll handle your dad."

"I'd appreciate it."

When Madelyn came running down the walk, duffel bag over her shoulder, overnight case bobbing at her side and her face bright with the emotion of her paren-tal confrontations, a weird sensation enveloped Ty. The way the scene was set, they could have been eloping.

He kicked that thought right out of his mind. But it ran back in and wouldn't budge. And he knew why. Madelyn Gentry was a very sexy, very attractive woman, and though he might be discriminating he wasn't dead. He found her as attractive as any man would find her. And now that he'd seen three rows of neatly folded pink, red and black panties, he could form those pictures and images that wouldn't initially appear in his brain and she wasn't as safe with him as he'd thought.

So he reminded himself that he wasn't interested. First, she was too darned young for him. But, second, most women who pursued him only wanted his money. Madelyn, with dreams of establishing her own busi-ness, would be no exception. In fact, now that he thought about it, her financial situation was a lot like his former fiancée Anita's had been when he met her. Wrestling with a failing business, Anita had impressed him as being tough and determined, so he'd happily lent her money....

He groaned, his hands forming fists on the steering wheel. That situation had ended abysmally. Anita hadn't merely made him a laughingstock by taking him to the cleaners financially. She'd cheated on him the whole time they dated. Worse, she'd also cost Ty a brother. When Cooper discovered Anita was cheating, he'd warned Ty, but Ty had accused Cooper of using the information to manipulate him. By the time the truth came out that Anita was the one manipulating him and Cooper had been right about her cheating, Cooper was long gone. He'd packed his bags and moved to parts unknown and they hadn't seen him since.

Ty ran his hand down his face. That was a point in his life that he didn't care to revisit, though he was glad he had. The fact that Madelyn was more than ten years his junior might not cool his libido, but her being totally broke like his former fiancée certainly did. And that knowledge would keep him the hell away from her.

Madelyn opened the passenger side door of the SUV. "All set."

He didn't say anything. Not a word. He and Madelyn had only gotten chummy out of necessity. He'd had to talk to her to form this alliance and figure out the nuances of the deal. But now that he had accepted the fact he had a baby, and had a solid idea of Madelyn's personality from her dealings with her dad, he knew how to handle both the baby and the new nanny.

So the conversation ended here. He had work to do when they got home tonight. Then there were telephone calls to occupy him tomorrow and file folders that would keep him amused on Sunday.

And Madelyn had a baby to care for. As far as Ty was concerned, they really were "all set."

Ty Bryant hadn't said a word to her during the drive to his house, but when they arrived at his understated Cape Cod and found the entire porch littered with boxes, he was suddenly talkative again.

"I don't suppose you know how to assemble a crib?"

Madelyn gaped at him. "Even if I could, am I supposed to balance Sabrina on my hip while I screw in the bolts?"

"I'm sure women in primitive cultures do it."

"And I'm sure men in primitive cultures build their own cribs. They don't order them from a department store."

"I didn't order this stuff from a department store. I have a friend whose wife has connections at…"

"Whatever! Just put the crib together while I go look for something to make for dinner."

She left him standing amid the baby things and, with Sabrina on her hip, went in search of supper. Unfortunately, she didn't even find a box of macaroni in his cupboards. Though she had to admit his house was interesting. Not what she'd expected. The cherrywood cabinets in the kitchen gleamed. The sitting room she stumbled upon as she tried to find her way back to the foyer had a neat yellow contemporary sofa and chair with heavy-wood end tables and a wall-sized entertainment unit that probably cost a bundle. The dining room housed a light oak table and hutch filled with sparkly stemware that looked like it was never used.

When she returned to the foyer, Ty was nowhere in sight, but she saw he had hauled everything in from the porch. The boxes and bags were scattered atop the sand-colored ceramic tile. But she was more interested in the foyer's newly painted white walls that were decorated with what appeared to be antique mirrors. She couldn't deny that Ty Bryant owned a nice house, but it wasn't as grand as she expected for a guy who ran a multimillion dollar business.

Because Ty was gone and so was the crib box, she assumed he was in the room he intended to use as a nursery, assembling the baby's bed. She climbed the stairs and walked toward the only open door. From the hall she could see the room already had a single bed and maple dresser. Thick gray carpeting covered the floor. It made sense to assume he was making a nursery from one of his guest rooms, which was good, but that didn't put food in the cupboards and she was hungry.

She entered talking. "Are you on some kind of starvation diet?"

Seeing him sitting on the floor, with his black jacket and tie removed and the sleeves of his white shirt rolled up to reveal muscular forearms, Madelyn stopped dead in her tracks. His very neat hair had become tousled and he looked so darned sexily rumpled that she lost her breath.

"No. If you didn't find any food to cook, it's because I usually eat out."

Juggling Sabrina on her hip, Madelyn considered it

very lucky that he didn't glance up as he spoke because she wasn't sure she could take her eyes off him. He was just plain yummy-looking.

When several seconds lapsed without her reply, he peered up at her. "What? No smart remark about my always eating out?"

She swallowed and quickly looked away, as if inspecting what he had done with the crib. "I'm ordering pizza."

He pretended to shudder. "Oh, that was scathing."

"I mean it."

He shrugged and went back to work, fitting the metal springs into the wooden sides of the crib.

"And you're paying."

"Fine," he said, as if *he* were doing *her* a huge favor.

Madelyn stared at him, not understanding how he could think he was doing her a favor, when this entire job was nothing but a favor from *her* to *him*. But she wasn't about to give him the satisfaction of letting him see he annoyed her. Rather than storm out as she might have done, she very casually walked out. Downstairs, she grabbed the wall phone in the kitchen and dialed the number for pizza delivery from memory, ordered what *she* wanted—to hell with his choice—and then rummaged through Sabrina's diaper bag so she could feed the baby first.

If he wanted to aggravate her day and night for the next three days, he had better be ready for the consequences. She had enough experience with her dad that she could take on any chauvinist, and in a perverse way she might even enjoy it. God knew, Ty's attitude helped her to forget how good-looking he was.

When the pizza arrived, Madelyn was bathing Sabrina for bed so she let Ty answer the front door. She took her time washing, drying and dressing the baby. Then, because Ty had assembled the crib, she set Sabrina in a safety seat while she snapped new sheets on the mattress, wondering how Ty knew what to get his friend's wife to order for the baby. But she stopped that thought. She'd bet her bottom dollar he called his friend and simply told him to tell his wife to order everything needed for a baby.

It must be nice.

By the time she had Sabrina tucked into bed, Madelyn had herself worked into a sufficient low-level anger from the day's events. She was sure her mood would keep her on her toes with her sarcastic boss so she would stop noticing he was too damned sexy for a grouch. But when she entered the kitchen and found him eating pizza at the round wooden table while he skimmed the newspaper, the whole scene felt so "normal" and so "right" that she was bombarded by images of them as a happy couple.

Sitting, she cursed her thoughts. Really. Because they came out of nowhere and they weren't welcome. She wasn't a teenager, envisioning herself with the town hunk. She was living with her boss to help him. And if the constant reminder that she was this man's employee didn't stop her fantasies, the man himself should. He had no place in a domestic daydream because he wasn't domesticated. Plus, men who liked sophisticated women really only wanted no-strings-attached sex. He was not her type. He wasn't *anybody's* type.

"Are you going to eat that pizza, or are you just going to sit there with your mouth open, staring at me?"

Great! Now he was noticing her staring at him. Somehow she had to get accustomed to him so she could keep herself in line. No, that wasn't it. What she had to do was get herself accustomed to the fact that she was *living with* a man who could be described as one of the sexiest guys on the face of the earth. Then she would be able to keep herself in line.

She tried to think of other sexy men she had spent time with and four names came to mind. Unfortunately, she'd dated one of them, only worked occasionally with the other two and nursed an awful crush on the fourth. But it had been okay to like those guys because none of them were arrogant. She couldn't deal with Ty the same way that she'd dealt with the others because Ty Bryant wasn't like anybody she knew.

Actually, that was both the truth and the real dilemma. Ty Bryant really was unlike anybody she'd ever met. He was handsome. He was smart. He was clearly clever to have built an empire singlehandedly. And he'd taken in a child. No matter how much Madelyn tried to downplay his caring for Sabrina by reminding herself that he was more or less forced to take the baby, she also knew he could have sent Sabrina to foster care. Of course, that really would make him an ogre—and he wasn't.

That was it!

That was the problem! Ty Bryant really wasn't an ogre as his employees thought. No matter how much he tormented her or made her mad, brief revelations of his nice side kept causing her to forget his bad side. So all she had to do was remember his bad side and she would be okay.

Just when she drew the conclusion that she could stop her pounding heart, daydreaming and inappropriate staring simply by reminding herself of all the impolite, self-centered, arrogant things she'd seen and heard Ty Bryant do in the past few hours, he rose from his seat.

From the way he swiped a napkin across his mouth, it appeared that he was done eating and leaving the kitchen. But when he stopped by her chair, Madelyn got her first tremor of unease. He caught her arm, hauled her up, spun her around and pressed his mouth to hers.

Madelyn knew that if she were ever going to faint in her life, this would be the minute. His mouth attacked hers, completely disarming her. She couldn't stop her arms from reaching up to encircle his shoulders. The sexual chemistry between them was so strong it led her, guided her, pulled her to do things without her conscious thought. But she didn't care. The kiss was so darned good she was more than happy to let it take her anywhere it wanted to go.

As quickly as he grabbed her, Ty let her loose and stepped back. Madelyn gazed up at him, too startled by the kiss to breathe, let alone speak.

But Ty didn't seem to have the same problem. "Watch yourself, Miss Maddy," he warned. "I'm a man who sees what he wants and takes it. If you're going to work for me, you either have to be able to accept the consequences of your subtle flirting, or you have to stop flirting."

"Flirting," Madelyn sputtered, confused, aroused, angry and unable to separate her emotions long enough to know which one she should trust.

"Yeah. Flirting. I kissed you so you would respond

and wouldn't be able to deny you're attracted to me, so we could get this darned thing out in the open. Deal with it. If you want to play sex games, I'll be more than happy to oblige. But I met your dad and I don't think he'd be too happy with that. I also met your mom, and I realized you're a lot like her. She's got a home, a family and a very steady man for a husband. Those are probably the things you want, too. And that means I'm not the guy you should be messing with."

With that he left the room, and Madelyn fell to her chair again, so embarrassed her face burned.

Chapter Three

The next morning, Madelyn wanted to punch something. Awake most of the night with a confused baby who sobbed nonstop because she missed her parents and didn't understand what was happening to her, Ty's temporary nanny wasn't in the mood to have to dress Sabrina and leave the house for bread, milk, eggs and coffee to make breakfast. She also needed to buy formula because Sabrina had only one bottle left of the batch Pete Hauser had provided. But Madelyn had to consult her mother before she made the formula purchase. Still her "boss" wasn't answering any of her knocks on his bedroom door and, as she had discovered the night before, his kitchen was bare.

Knowing her only recourse was to go in and physically wake him, she put her hand on the knob and almost twisted, but she suddenly realized it was very possible that he was as bare as his cupboards, sprawled across his bed like a naked Greek god.

Her chest tightened at the thought, and memories of the way he had kissed her the night before caused heat to flood through her. But so did her acute humiliation afterward. His kiss might have been so seductive it made her forget her own name, but he hadn't kissed her because he was attracted to her. He'd kissed her to make a point.

There was no way in hell she was going into his room to wake him. If he as much as insinuated she'd approached him for anything other than his help with the baby, she knew she couldn't be responsible for her actions. She'd absolutely deck him.

Sabrina squealed.

"Yeah, honey, we have to go out," she told the little girl who should have been as tired as Madelyn, but seemed to have the stamina of a navy SEAL. The baby gurgled a response and Madelyn turned away from Ty's bedroom door, determined she would never again let her attraction for that man show.

He was soooo safe with her, Madelyn thought, dressing the baby for the trip outside. After his arrogance the night before, she doubted she was even attracted to him anymore. She didn't like arrogant men. No smart woman did. She would happily stay so far away from him he wouldn't even have to worry about talking to her.

Madelyn found a spare set of keys for the SUV hanging on a bulletin board in the mudroom and twenty-three dollars casually strewn on a coffee table, probably money he'd taken from his pocket the night before. She didn't feel she was stealing. She was stocking *his* damned cupboards. She certainly wasn't using her own money. In fact, if she ever did have to spend her own money on things for the house or the baby, she was expensing it!

After buckling Sabrina in the car seat, Madelyn drove to a nearby convenience store. She purchased the items she needed, holding Sabrina on her hip because if there was a stroller in the stack of baby items that still littered the foyer, Ty hadn't yet put it together. She juggled the milk, eggs, bread, coffee and baby on the way to the checkout counter and had only a little more success carrying everything after the clerk put her purchases into bags. Maneuvering the baby and the bags on her left hand and arm, she opened the SUV door, then dumped the groceries on the passenger-side seat and fastened Sabrina in again.

By the time she returned to Ty Bryant's kitchen, she was exhausted, frazzled and not a woman to be trifled with. So, when she found Ty sitting at the kitchen table as if life were good and easy, and he said, "There you are," as if she'd stolen his SUV, it took every ounce of her control not to throttle him.

She sucked in a slow breath, ignoring the sizzle of attraction that zipped through her simply at the sight of him. Dressed in jeans and a T-shirt, with his hair sexily tousled and his eyes bright from sufficient sleep, he was about as good looking as a man could be. But making that observation also made her angry with herself for being attracted to a jerk who not only humiliated her the night before, but also considered that she might have stolen his car.

"I went to the store." Balancing Sabrina on her hip, Madelyn set the groceries on the table.

"Great, I'm starving."

"Me, too," she said casually, making good on her promise to herself that he would never have to worry about her attraction again, though she couldn't deny that he looked darned good. Maybe too good. His jeans and T-shirt hugged muscles his suit hid. But more than that, he didn't have the appearance or demeanor of a man who had just awakened. His movements weren't slow or sluggish. His eyes were sharp and focused.

The thought that he might have been awake, in his room, ignoring her knocks, caused anger to career through Madelyn like a runaway eighteen-wheeler. Still, she wasn't about to do anything foolish, and yelling at him for something that couldn't be changed would be. But she could most certainly guide his future behavior and how this household would operate from now on.

"After you make a pot of coffee, why don't you scramble some eggs for both of us and make toast while I feed Sabrina."

He peered at her as if she'd suggested he put on a dress and stand in Porter's town square and Madelyn felt her spine stiffen and strength ooze to her limbs, as indignation prepared her for a fight. She might not do anything foolish, but she would correct him if he dared tell her no.

"I hope that puzzled look doesn't mean you think I should be the one doing the cooking."

"No," he said slowly, prudently as far as Madelyn was concerned. "It's just that I don't cook. I can make the coffee but I wouldn't guarantee an egg."

"Sounds like you've got some learning to do then."

Madelyn knew she had to get the heck out of the room. She was tired and short-tempered. But more than that, he was starting to look good to her again. And that simply wasn't right.

She pushed through the swinging door that took her to a short hall that led to the stairway. In the nursery, she fed Sabrina the last bottle in the group Pete Hauser had brought to Ty's office, and like a miracle the little girl fell asleep. Madelyn laid her in her crib and gazed longingly at the single bed she'd slept on for about twenty minutes the night before.

A wise woman would take her sleep time when she could, but Madelyn had to call her mother to ask about the appropriate formula for a six-month-old baby and purchase a supply before the baby awakened. Plus, she hadn't forgotten the other end of this deal. She had to get Ty actively involved in her PR ideas while he needed her or she knew he wouldn't do half the things required to improve his reputation.

She left the nursery and made her way to the kitchen. Pushing through the swinging door, she found her boss making toast.

"You don't by any chance like your toast black?"

"No. If you burned some, those are yours."

"Great," he said, also prudently.

He would have to be a complete idiot not to notice she was cranky. Nonetheless, she gave him points for recognizing when to back off, and she softened her tone when she said, "I came up with a few more PR things last night." She grabbed a piece of toast on the way to the cupboard to get a mug. The coffee smelled incredibly strong, but Madelyn didn't care. The extra caffeine would come in handy.

Ty turned back to the toaster. "I assume Sabrina's

resting, so why don't you take this free time to type them up. I'll look at them when I get a chance."

That felt so much like a brush-off that Madelyn stopped the coffeepot midpour. "What's wrong with hearing me out now?"

"I have things to do this morning. I make my schedule a week in advance. Since I didn't know I'd be getting a baby on Friday, I have tons of things that have to be done today or I'm screwed."

Again, Madelyn felt like she was being brushed off, but she recognized that people who ran companies the size of Ty's typically had hellish schedules. She also knew her sour mood was coloring her judgment. But before she could comment, Ty grabbed two pieces of toast and a cup of coffee and left the kitchen without another word.

Madelyn blew her breath out on a long sigh and rose to retrieve the receiver for the wall phone. Though, technically, he was breaking their agreement, she had things to handle for the baby. So this wasn't the time to push him about the PR arrangement.

"It's me, Mom," Madelyn said when her mother answered the phone. "I need some help. Sabrina is out of formula and there aren't any notes or anything in the diaper bag Ty got from the lawyer who gave him the baby."

"How old is she?"

"Six months."

Penney Gentry instructed her daughter on how to choose a temporary formula for the baby, but added, "You really should find out who her pediatrician is and call him to see what he knows about Sabrina."

"I haven't even slept yet, Mom. I doubt that I have the strength to talk to her doctor. Besides it's Saturday."

Madelyn's mom didn't say anything for a second, then she asked, "Are you okay?"

"Just tired."

"How about if your dad and I get the formula and bring it to the house?"

"How about if you do it alone?"

Penney laughed. "Your dad is fine. He was just a bit concerned last night. Ty Bryant doesn't have a very good reputation."

Ha! Didn't Madelyn know the truth of that! She was the one charged with fixing the impression the whole town had that Ty Bryant was one of Satan's minions. "His reputation is as a scrooge, Mom, not a philanderer. I'm safe." She rolled her eyes. If her mother only knew how safe she was!

"I suppose." Penney sighed. "It's just that when somebody isn't nice in one way it's not a stretch to think they're into other things, too."

"Like he's a scrooge who seduces young women?" Madelyn said, then she laughed. "Trust me, Mom. The guy's not interested. And even if he were, we're both too busy. Between the baby and trying to figure out how to clean up Ty's reputation—which, by the way, even you know and you never met the guy until yesterday—I've got my hands full."

"All right. I'll try to ditch your dad and be there in about an hour or so."

"Thanks. And Mom…" Madelyn wound the phone cord around her finger, not quite sure she should make her next statement since it was her job to convince people Ty Bryant wasn't an ogre or scrooge. She drew a quick breath and plunged in anyway. "Get a receipt and use the back door."

Her mother laughed. "Oh, honey, your work is so cut out for you."

Madelyn desperately wanted to nap for the hour it would take her mom to get the formula, but the call with her mother reinforced how important it was to clean up Ty's image. That meant she had to get her PR ideas typed up so she could get Ty involved *now*. But on her way to his office to get the laptop computer, Madelyn saw the foyer full of baby things.

She sighed. It would be easier for her to have all the baby clothes, diapers and crib sheets upstairs. Plus, a mobile on the crib might soothe Sabrina back to sleep at night. Not only that, but Madelyn needed the stroller.

She sighed again. Because getting Sabrina settled and happy would ultimately free up more time to work on the PR, she decided to take it one box at a time. She would put away the clothes, diapers and crib sheets, then install the mobile and assemble the stroller. But that was as far as she was going. Ty was the baby's guardian. He would do the rest of this.

Her mother hadn't arrived after an hour of unpacking. Madelyn checked on Sabrina to make sure she was still sleeping soundly and made her way to Ty's den for the computer. He sat at his desk, engrossed in a report. She slid the laptop from his file cabinet, expecting him to question her, but he didn't as much as look up. He had to know she was there. Yet, he ignored her.

Well, peachy. He didn't want to talk to her. Big deal. She didn't want to talk to him either. The only conversation they needed was about PR and Sabrina. She most certainly didn't want to get accused of flirting with him again. So fine. He could be silent as much as he wanted. It worked for her.

At the kitchen table, she typed out the notes of the PR strategies she'd come up with the night before. Another hour went by before her mother knocked on the back door.

She jumped up and ran to answer it. But when she pulled open the door, it was her dad she faced. "Hey, Miss Maddy."

"Hey, Dad," she said, struggling to keep the panic out of her voice. "Where's Mom?"

Her mom peeked out from behind her dad. "Here."

"You couldn't convince him to stay home, could you?"

"Now, see here, young lady. It's my job to be concerned."

"I told Mom there was nothing to worry about."

"Give me a minute to look around and see that for myself, and I won't be back again unless you ask me." He stepped into the kitchen, Maddy's mom on his heels.

Madelyn closed the door. "Dad, it's not like I'm staying here forever."

"Oh?" Maddy's mom said, as Ron Gentry set the grocery bag containing the baby's formula on the table and Penney slipped off her sweater, an indication she intended to stay. Madelyn almost told her not to get too cozy, but her mother said, "So, Mr. Bryant called a nanny service last night, then?"

"No," Madeline said. She'd been so embarrassed by him kissing her that she'd forgotten all about that.

"Then how do you know you're coming home soon?"

"I'll have him call today."

"Right," her dad said, glancing around. "Where's the baby?"

"Sleeping."

Maddy's mom glanced at her watch. "Goodness, Maddy, I hope she hasn't been sleeping all morning after being awake all night!"

"Actually, she has."

"Oh, honey, get her up right now or she's going to have her days and nights mixed up and you'll never get any sleep."

"Won't be her worry if she actually gets Mr. Scrooge to use some of his moldy money to hire a nanny instead of tricking an employee into caring for his baby for nothing."

The way her dad said that caused a fission of alarm to skitter through Madelyn. Could Ty have tricked her out of getting him to call the nanny service the night before because he didn't want to spend the money? It seemed so ridiculous that she refused to entertain it. But her dad's comment did demonstrate how easily everything Ty did could be misinterpreted.

"Anything else you need our help with?" her dad asked.

Madelyn almost automatically said no, but she remembered that Ty hadn't put together the high chair or baby swing, and she needed both of them. "Actually," she said, directing her dad to follow her to the door, "There are some things we haven't yet assembled."

"You mean the illustrious Mr. Bryant hasn't assembled," Ron said, following Maddy. When she cast him a curious look, he said, "You're not exactly a pro with a screwdriver, so I knew you hadn't volunteered."

Madelyn grimaced as she pushed open the swinging door and began walking down the hall to the foyer where the boxes still lay on the floor. "Come on, Dad. He's a busy man and this baby was just sort of dropped in his lap yesterday. He didn't have time to—"

Seeing Ty sitting on the floor, among the boxes, with the high chair pieces neatly arranged for assembly, Madelyn stopped walking.

"Mr. and Mrs. Gentry," he greeted coolly, but politely, when he looked up from the parts he had sorted.

"I was just bringing my dad in to put the high chair together."

"I can handle it," Ty said and went back to work.

Madelyn glanced at her dad and saw his look of puzzlement turn into a look of pleasure. Seeing Ty dressed in jeans and a T-shirt, with a screwdriver in his hand, looking like a common, ordinary guy, her dad seemed to have upped his impression of Porter's most disliked citizen a million decimal places.

"Are you sure you don't want any help?" Ron said, using his guy-to-guy voice and Madelyn knew her conclusion was correct. Ty had scored big time. "I'm not busy today. I'd be glad to hang around a while."

"I'm fine," Ty said, then he paused, glanced up at her dad and said, "But thanks."

Madelyn stared in amazement as a strange feeling billowed through her. The little bits of kindness she saw creep into Ty's personality were so subtle she sometimes wondered if she imagined them, but she knew she hadn't imagined that. Ty saying thanks to her dad caused her to remember how polite he had been to her dad the day before when she introduced them and also to realize that Ty had let her make the explanation to her father. He hadn't interrupted her or even hurried her. He'd stood by politely and let her state her case. He wasn't rude. He wasn't abrupt.

And now that she thought about it, he was also pulling his weight with Sabrina. He might have seemed unhappy to be forced to make breakfast, but though he burned the toast, he had made it.

And at one point the night before, didn't she have the feeling that he was deliberately baiting her, aggravating her, trying to make her mad?

Yes, she had. She knew she had.

Could it be that his scrooge, ogre, tyrant personality was an act? After all, he'd said he'd worked fifteen years to get his reputation.

"You're welcome," Ron said cheerfully, bringing Madelyn out of her thoughts.

She turned her parents around and directed them toward the kitchen. "You guys better go now."

"I could help," Ron said one more time, as the kitchen door swung closed behind them.

"He doesn't really want help," Madelyn reminded her dad as she guided him and her mother to the back door. "He *wants* to put the baby's things together."

"Well, good," Penney said. She stopped at the table to retrieve her sweater. "One of the most important things Mr. Bryant needs to understand is that he's that baby's family now. Even when he gets a nanny he has to be involved with Sabrina. It's good to see he's not passing off her care."

"Right," Madelyn agreed, seeing her own image of Ty altering. Though he hadn't yet changed a diaper, he was putting together the much-needed baby equipment.

He wasn't shirking his responsibility with the baby. He was simply doing the things he knew how to do and also fitting them into an already busy schedule. Giving him the benefit of the doubt, she said, "He isn't passing off the baby's care completely."

Her mother beamed. "That's so good to hear."

Her parents stepped out into the early-afternoon sunshine and Madelyn closed the door behind them, feeling victorious. Maybe mending Ty's image wouldn't be so bad after all? Merely seeing him with a screwdriver had sold her dad. And all her mom had to do was hear that Ty was involved with the baby, and her disposition shifted, too. Of course, Madelyn had sort of lied about Ty being involved with the baby. But she would fix that this afternoon.

Reminded that she needed to awaken the baby, Madelyn ran up the back stairs and into the temporary nursery.

"Sabrina," she called, gently lifting the little girl from her crib. "Sabrina, honey, you've got to wake up."

Sabrina rubbed her nose on Madelyn's shoulder, found a comfortable spot and went back to sleep and Madelyn didn't have the heart to wake her.

"Okay. All right," Madelyn said, laying her down again. Sabrina had lost both of her parents the week before. She'd had enough traumas to last her a while.

"We'll let you sleep now, but tonight your Uncle Ty is playing with you so you can't fall asleep until you're good and darned tired."

Having Ty directly care for Sabrina that night would solve both the baby sleeping problem and the little white lie she'd told her mother.

She returned to the computer at the kitchen table and began detailing the new ideas she had gotten for making Ty seem more like a normal guy from her father's reaction to seeing him put together a high chair. When she ran out of steam, she considered going into the foyer to check on Ty's progress with the baby things, but decided against it. He had accused her of flirting, and though she hadn't flirted, she probably had been staring at him, so it was best for her to keep her distance. Besides, having formula ready when the baby woke was a better use of her time.

A half hour later when she heard the baby cry, she got Sabrina out of bed, fed her a little of the cereal from the box Pete had sent in the diaper bag, and then went in search of Ty. Though he wasn't in the foyer, the high chair was assembled. So was the swing. But all the other boxes were intact.

Not sure where he was, but knowing he had probably given her all the free time he could spare for one day, Madelyn headed down the hall to his den.

"There's your Uncle Ty," Madelyn said talking to the baby as she entered the room.

Ty slowly looked up from his work. "I told you I have things I have to accomplish today."

"Yes, but this is your child now, and I'm not your wife," she said, then batted down an odd reaction that shivered through her at the thought of getting his sizzling kisses regularly. There was no way in hell she would marry a grouch, and besides, this particular grouch wasn't interested in her.

"Which means I'm really not her permanent caregiver. After losing her parents and being shifted away from her grandparents, you don't want her to get attached to me and lose me, too."

Ty tossed his pencil to his desk. "No, I suppose I don't." Madelyn almost cheered, until he added, "But right now I'm swamped. In February, Seth lost a contract for a twenty-million-dollar mansion in Florida. The owner, foreign royalty, paid us for all the work we did, but he never gave us a reason for firing us and he also didn't pay us the amount in the termination clause. The way he handled this, it was as if we'd quit on him, he hadn't fired us."

"Oh," Madelyn said, taking a seat on the chair in front of his desk and arranging Sabrina on her lap.

"So, we sued this king."

"You sued a *king?*"

"He didn't keep to the terms of our agreement."

"You're not afraid of repercussions?"

"That's just it. There weren't any. After one preliminary hearing the king buckled under and agreed to pay us the amount in the termination clause of the contract."

Madelyn nodded.

"Problem is," Ty said softly, almost contritely, "he sent a twenty-page agreement for us to sign to settle the suit. I have to read it today so that if I make any changes the legal department has time to insert them and we can present our version to our former client."

Madelyn was nearly speechless at Ty's humble, apologetic tone until she remembered this was how he got her to agree to be his temporary nanny in the first place. She almost argued that he couldn't put his business before the baby, but she remembered it was more important for him to care for the baby that night. And if she won this battle with him right now, she would actually lose the help she needed from him that evening.

"Okay," she said, rising. "I'll care for Sabrina this afternoon, and you get her tonight."

He considered that, then said, "Okay."

"You also need to call a nanny service."

"Okay," he agreed amicably.

Madelyn left Ty's office and walking through the foyer, she saw the newly assembled high chair and baby swing and realized she needed one in the kitchen and the other in the TV room. Juggling Sabrina from one arm to the other, Madelyn concluded she couldn't carry either the swing or the high chair while she held the baby. So she set the baby in the swing and carried the high chair to the kitchen, then put Sabrina in the high chair while she carried the swing to the TV room.

The entire time that she carried baby items, ordered another pizza for a midafternoon snack since they'd missed lunch, and amused the little girl who was raring to go, Madelyn didn't hear a sound from Ty. But because he had agreed to care for the baby that night, Madelyn didn't bother him. At six o'clock when he emerged from his den, looking for "anything" to eat, Madelyn was incredibly happy to see him.

"Thank God!" she said, pulling Sabrina out of the high chair and handing her to Ty. "Do you realize I haven't even showered today?"

"You should get up earlier," Ty said, shifting away as if he didn't see her handing him the baby.

Madelyn frowned. "You can't get up much earlier than two in the morning."

He took a piece of pizza and sat at the table. "Why the hell would you get up at two?"

She stared at him. "Because *your baby*," she said, accenting those words because she was starting to worry she had given him too much benefit of the doubt. "Got up at two and stayed up until right after I came back from the convenience store."

He said, "Hum," and reached for the morning paper again.

"Ty," she said, using his first name to snag his attention. When he looked up, she said, "I'm getting the impression you're missing the big picture."

"And what would that picture be?"

His voice dripped with strained patience and she almost laughed. If he thought his nerves were strained, he should get a look at hers!

"That you are this baby's guardian."

"That's not something I'll easily forget."

"Maybe you won't forget it, but you're not acting like a guardian."

"I see. You don't want to do the nanny work, so you're dumping it off on me."

"I stayed up all night with this baby while you slept. I took her to the store while you slept…"

"I wasn't sleeping. I was up at six. Working."

"You were up at six yet you never volunteered to help me?"

"*You're* the nanny!"

"*You're* the baby's guardian! Dear God, Ty, are you going to make her live like a pet? No, I take that back, most people's pets get more attention. You've all but ignored this little girl."

For a few seconds Ty just stared at her, then he quietly said, "In order to be able to support that little girl, I have work to do. That's why we made this arrangement. If you don't like it, there's the door. But, remember, if you leave, you don't do the PR."

At that moment, walking out the door and never looking back sounded like a fine deal to Madelyn. But in twenty-four hours of caring for the baby, remembering Sabrina had lost both of her parents, remembering she'd been taken away from everybody and everything familiar, Madelyn had grown to love her and couldn't desert her to a man who didn't even acknowledge her existence.

She didn't know how she would do it, but somehow, some way, she would get this stubborn, self-centered, self-oriented, tunnel-visioned, chauvinistic, completely-incapable-of-affection man to love this baby.

"I'll stay."

He smiled triumphantly and turned his gaze to the newspaper again. "I thought so."

Righteous indignation thundered through Madelyn. Before he'd said that she was miffed. Now she was mad. He was in for trouble the likes of which he'd never seen before.

Chapter Four

Monday morning as Ty stepped into his charcoal-gray trousers, he heard the baby crying. He zipped and buttoned quickly, then walked to the bedroom where he'd set up Sabrina's crib.

He wasn't a complete idiot. He knew what Madelyn had been telling him Saturday evening. Caring for a baby was hard and she wasn't a professional. She was simply somebody who knew enough to help him get over the rough spots. She couldn't handle being up all night and caring for the baby all day and still do the PR work she wanted to do.

Though that *was* the job she'd agreed to.

Still, he'd heard her walking the floor with the baby in the hours before anybody's alarm was scheduled to ring, and he understood that nobody could function without sleep three days in a row. So, in order to have at least a semipleasant person running his house while he went to work, he would handle some of the morning baby things and let her sleep in.

Standing over the crib, he said, "Hey, kid. You want to keep the noise down?"

Sabrina stopped crying and Ty smiled. There. That wasn't so hard. He sometimes believed women made caring for babies much more complicated than it needed to be. He reached in to pull Sabrina out, but as he did, she started to cry again.

"Oh, come on!" he said, bringing her nose almost to his nose. She angled her pajama-covered feet on his white undershirt. "You don't have two skilled professionals here," he told the baby who again stopped crying and only looked at him. "You've got to cut us a break."

Sabrina slapped his face. Twice. Then two more times before Ty realized she wasn't hitting him as much as his face was in the way of her getting out some pent-up energy. He couldn't believe she had any energy left after being up all night—especially considering that her "nanny" was a lifeless lump under the covers on the bed—and he decided he had made the right decision by handling some of the morning duties so Madelyn could sleep.

He went downstairs to get a bottle out of the refrigerator. Having seen Madelyn feed Sabrina, he knew at least the basics. After warming it, he laid the baby in the crook of his elbow and popped the nipple into her mouth as he headed upstairs again. He might want to give Madelyn a few extra minutes of sleep, but feeling a damp spot forming on his undershirt from Sabrina's soggy diaper, he realized that wasn't practical.

He walked over to Madelyn's bed and stared down

at her. She was sleeping so soundly and he was so well aware that she hadn't gotten any rest again the night before that he didn't have the heart to wake her.

The weakness made him mad. Damn it! This was her job! He didn't have time for this and he most certainly wasn't dressed for it. If he didn't do something soon his Armani trousers would be the next victim of Sabrina's leaky diaper.

He leaned over and whispered, "Madelyn?" as if waking her with a soft voice somehow made it okay. But, bent close to her face, he could see the perfection of her pale complexion, her pert little nose and her full lips.

He swallowed, remembering what it felt like to kiss those lips. He'd intended to prove a point to her, but ended up proving a point to both of them. They had chemistry. Wonderful chemistry for two people who could become lovers, but wickedly bad chemistry for an old man with a young woman who had to live together in his house for God knew how long. Particularly since said woman had a suspicious dad who'd already come over on Saturday, probably to check up on Ty.

Remembering punch-first-ask-questions-later Ron Gentry, Ty pulled back from the bed and decided to finish feeding the baby before he woke Madelyn. He didn't want to get on the bad side of her dad, but also, making the proactive choice to feed the baby as opposed to the negative choice of *not waking* the nanny wasn't so much a weakness as a matter of practicality. Madelyn needed sleep and Ty had more or less created a deadline. When the kid was fed, Madelyn would be awakened. As for the wetness currently seeping downward toward… He'd burn the trousers.

Sabrina gulped down her bottle in what Ty considered record time. After he set the empty on a nightstand, Ty and his damp trousers turned to the bed where Madeline slept. Again, regret for having to wake her swamped him, but when that guilt nearly had him turning away, he stopped himself.

He decided to look at this from Madelyn's point of view. She behaved like someone who really wanted to succeed, and as someone who had struggled from a position at the bottom himself, Ty knew that anybody seeking true success had to work harder than most people were willing to work and do things most people weren't willing to do. If this PR "kid" wanted to reach the top, there were dues to pay. And *this* was where she paid them. If Ty didn't wake her, he would be cheating her out of an opportunity to prove herself.

That was much better.

Properly motivated to wake her, Ty moved to the bed, leaned down and accidentally sniffed the scent of something floral as he again noticed how soft she looked. And peaceful. So needy of the rest she was getting that his compassion took over again and he could not wake her.

Damn it! What the hell was happening to him?

Luckily, Sabrina suffered from no qualm of conscience about waking her caregiver. She shrieked, probably as unhappy with her wet diaper as Ty was, and without thinking Ty nuzzled her to settle her down. "Shhh."

Madelyn stirred, and Ty glanced from the baby to Madelyn and back to the baby. Realizing again that Sabrina had no problem waking Madelyn, Ty nuzzled

Sabrina, bringing her close so he could whisper in her ear, "I'm sorry. I spoke that *shhh* too soon. You go ahead and complain. Your diaper's wet and leaking. You've got to be miserable. Let's hear it."

Madelyn awakened to see Ty standing over her, holding the baby, whispering something that made the little girl giggle and pat his face. Her first thought was to wonder how long he'd been standing there watching her sleep, which stirred a whirlwind of emotions inside her. The one she expected was attraction. He *was* luscious wearing only an undershirt and gray trousers, and it was simply too early in the morning to battle down any instinctive roller-coaster ride her tummy and heart might take. The emotion she hadn't expected, though, and the one that was infinitely more difficult to deal with, was a kind of joy. Ty was behaving very sweetly with the baby and for some reason—also too early in the morning to dissect—that pleased her enormously.

Cuddling Sabrina, Ty had the air of a man bonding with his baby. He appeared at ease and comfortable starting the day in a private moment with the little girl he had been entrusted to raise. In fact, the whole room was bathed in intimacy. Wrapped in warm covers, watching him nuzzle Sabrina, Madelyn felt very much like a wife watching her husband. And it didn't seem wrong, or even inappropriate. It seemed absolutely normal.

Because that feeling was dead wrong and also more than a little bit stupid, Madelyn shifted her attention away from herself and Ty, and put it back where it belonged. On Ty and his child. His nuzzling Sabrina appeared effortless. His loose, yet protective hold was instinctive. The way he blew on her neck, teasing and playing, wasn't something that could be taught. From those simple things it was clear to Madelyn that baby care would come to this man naturally, if he would only spend some time with Sabrina.

Madelyn's hopes for her boss skyrocketed, until he glanced down and saw she was awake.

"There you are," he said, and virtually dropped the baby on Madelyn's stomach. "I'm late."

With that he pivoted and strode out of the room as Madelyn grabbed the wobbling baby to keep her from rolling to the floor.

So much for celebrating Ty's instincts.

But at least she knew he had them. And she wasn't letting *him* forget. In fact, seeing how easily baby care seemed to come to him fortified her resolve to put "Operation: Baby Love" into effect.

After Ty ran out of the house for work, Madelyn put Sabrina in the baby seat and set it on the floor just beyond the half-open curtain of the shower so she could begin dressing for the day. She had just wrapped herself in a thick terry cloth robe when her mother entered the front door.

"Madelyn?" she called up the steps.

"Mom?"

Her dad called, "Are you decent?"

"Yes."

Then both parents clambered up the steps and invaded her bedroom simultaneously.

"I'll take the baby," her dad said.

"No, I'll take the baby," her mother argued. "She needs to be bathed and dressed. I can do that while Madelyn puts on that pretty blue suit you have in your hands."

Ron handed the suit to Madelyn. "So what do *I* do?"

"Well, since you're here, I would love some toast," Madelyn ventured sheepishly.

"Okay. Okay," Ron said as he left the room.

Madelyn and her mother worked quickly to get both Madelyn and the baby dressed. Then Madelyn gobbled a piece of toast and took her car keys from her mother. "Did you get the car seat Arlene left in the garage?"

"Yep. It's already installed."

"I did that," her dad said.

"Good," Madelyn said, lifting the carrier that held Sabrina. "Diaper bag?"

"Check." Penney slid the tightly packed blue plaid monstrosity onto Madelyn's free shoulder. "You're all set to go."

"Wish me luck."

"Luck," her dad said as she walked to the door. "I have a feeling you're going to need it."

So did Madelyn, but she wasn't backing down. First, if it killed her she would get Ty to love his new baby. Second, she had a job to do, too. The CEO of Bryant Development might have forgotten that she now had less than three weeks to get him ready for a *Wall Street Journal* interview even as she turned around his image to the residents of Porter, Arkansas, but Madelyn hadn't. She intended to do this job and she intended to do it very, very well.

Ten minutes later, she stepped into the lobby of the Bryant Building. Three stories high and with a skylight that lit the entryway, the open area contained only a cherrywood desk and a semicircle of thickly padded wheat-colored leather chairs.

"Hello, Ginny," Madelyn called to the receptionist.

Short and thin with glossy brown hair and a personality every bit as bright, Ginny glanced up from the letter she was proofreading. "Hey, Madelyn, who have you got there?" she asked as she bent across her desk to look down at Sabrina who was sitting in the baby carrier that Madelyn held loosely at her side.

"This is Sabrina Bryant." Madelyn set the baby seat on Ginny's desk. "Ty got custody of his cousin's baby Friday afternoon."

Ginny nodded her understanding. "This must be Scotty's little girl."

"Yes. Ty and I were having a meeting when Pete Hauser brought her in. Joni had already gone for the day, so I got elected to help Ty care for Sabrina while he looks for a nanny."

"Good idea," Ginny agreed. The baby screeched and banged her rattle against the protective loop of padding that held her in. Ginny laughed. "She's a noisy one."

Madelyn rolled her eyes. "You should hear her at 3:00 a.m."

Ginny laughed with delight. "I'd pay to see Tyrant Ty at 3:00 a.m. with this kid screaming in his ear."

"Now, Ginny, Ty's actually very good with her."

"I'd have to see that myself."

"You *will* see him with Sabrina. We have no choice but to bring her to work until he gets a nanny. You'll have plenty of chances to see him with the baby."

With that, Madelyn walked through the reception area and to the elevator. She stepped in, pushed the button for the second floor and then took a deep breath. "We're in now, Sabrina. Once the receptionist knows something, there's no taking it back. So we might as well keep going."

Sabrina cooed and grinned toothlessly.

"Right. I hope your new daddy is as happy about it as you are." The elevator slowed to a stop. Madelyn hoisted the baby about nose level and whispered, "This is accounting. I'll need to see some real personality from you here because these guys won't laugh as easily as Ginny did. Can you give me some personality?"

Sabrina screeched joyously.

"That's my girl."

An hour later, Madelyn arrived at the group of rooms that comprised Ty's office suite. "Good morning, Joni."

"Good morning, Madelyn," Joni said, looking up from her computer. "Oh, you have the baby!"

"Yeah. What's Ty doing?"

Joni pointed at the conference room to the right of Ty's office. "Executive staff meeting."

"Great. I need to be there anyway."

Joni's eyes rounded and became huge. "You can't go in there!"

"Why not? I have some things I need to tell the department managers. Besides, it's been about two hours since Ty's seen the baby. He's going to want me to bring her in."

Joni looked totally perplexed. "He'll *want* a baby in executive staff?"

"Well, he may not 'want' her in executive staff, but we don't have much choice. He couldn't hire a nanny over a weekend, too much background checking to be done, and he also realizes that Sabrina's going to have to spend time with him to get adjusted to him, so we're sort of killing two birds with one stone by bringing her to work."

Joni only stared at Madelyn.

"He's really not quite the grouch everybody thinks he is."

Joni laughed heartily.

Madelyn said, "You'll see." Then she opened the door to Ty's private conference room and prepared to ignore or—more appropriately—"spin" whatever reaction she got from Ty.

Standing at the head of the conference table, dressed in a dark blue suit and pale blue shirt, he looked gorgeous and Madelyn's breath caught and her knees wobbled. Just the sight of him caused her pulse rate to triple. He was simply a sexy, heart-stopping man and she realized Ty's reaction to the baby wasn't the only reaction she was going to have to spin.

"Whew!" she said, setting Sabrina's baby seat on the foot of conference room table, pretending to be tired, not bowled over by Ty's good looks. The heads of eight department managers turned Madelyn's way. One by one she watched their eyes widen, jaws slacken and mouths fall open. "This is Sabrina."

Sandy-haired, green-eyed Seth Bryant rose from his seat beside Ty's place at the head of the table. "Scotty's little girl?"

Ty took a slow breath and caught Madelyn's gaze. She saw absolutely nothing in his coal-black eyes. Not amusement. Not anger. Damn. He had to give her something to "spin" or she was going to fall flat on her face.

Finally, he quietly said, "Yes, Seth, that's Scotty's daughter. Pete Hauser brought her in Friday afternoon."

Seth slowly walked toward the baby. When he reached the foot of the table, though, he held back. Still, Madelyn almost expected that. Seth was a quiet, withdrawn man. From what she'd gathered from gossip, Seth had been a real philanderer. A wild card. The Bryant everybody loved. But after losing a contract—which Madelyn now knew was the Florida mansion contract—people said he'd become quiet and subdued.

"She's cute."

"Would you like to hold her?" Madelyn prodded.

He pulled back. "I've never actually held a baby before."

"Neither had Ty," Madeline assured him. "But he took to her like a pro."

The gazes of the seven remaining department heads shot to Ty, who sighed heavily. "Ms. Gentry, in case you missed it, I'm having a meeting here."

"Yeah, I know. Executive staff," Madelyn said as she unbuckled the strap that was looped over Sabrina's shoulders and Seth quietly made his way back to his seat. "I thought you could hold Sabrina while I brief everyone on the *Wall Street Journal* interview that's coming up." She lifted Sabrina out of the seat.

"And exactly why would *you* need to brief them?"

"So, they're aware of what's going to happen," Madelyn said as she handed Sabrina to Ty, all but forcing him to take her. The move got Madelyn's desired effect, though. When Ty didn't let Sabrina drop to the floor, and quite naturally settled her into the crook of his arm, all eight department managers, including Ty's own brother, gaped at him.

Madelyn turned to face the group, as if nothing were amiss. "I have a reporter from the *Wall Street Journal* coming in three weeks. Chances are he'll want to interview some of you. Be honest. If he asks to speak with your staff, let him."

Though Madelyn expected a gasp at that, no one uttered a sound. She was just about certain they were in shock. Not only was Ty Bryant holding a baby, but also they'd just been instructed to let their staff speak to the press. Obviously, both were unheard of here at Bryant Development.

"I want the reporter to have access to anybody he wishes to speak with, if only to show him this company has nothing to hide."

"Madelyn—" Seth began, but Madelyn interrupted him.

"I'm sorry, Seth, did I misinterpret something when you hired me? Does Bryant Development have something to hide?"

All eyes shifted to Ty. He stood off to Madelyn's right, holding the baby who was currently banging a rattle against his shoulder. They looked at him. He looked at them. No one said a word.

"Okay, then," Madelyn said, deliberately ignoring the fact that everybody, even Ty, believed he should be hidden from the *Wall Street Journal* reporter, as she reached to take Sabrina from Ty. "That's all I needed to tell you. If anybody has any questions for me, I'll be in my office."

She walked to the foot of the conference table. Holding Sabrina over the baby seat, she gasped as if she'd forgotten something. "I'm sorry, Ty. I just assumed you would want me to take Sabrina with me to my office. Did you want to keep her here?"

He said only, "No."

Madelyn set Sabrina in the baby carrier and buckled her in. His answer wasn't a perfect response but it was good enough. "I'll see you tonight, then." She paused on her way out the door. "Oh, unless you'd like to have lunch with the baby?"

This "no" was a little firmer and Madelyn got his message loud and clear that she was pushing things. Whatever. As long as Ty didn't out-and-out yell, Madelyn knew she was making points with his staff.

That night when Ty returned home, he methodically searched his house for Madelyn. He found neither nanny nor baby, but he did discover a mouthwatering pot roast in the oven. The scent made his stomach growl.

"My parents shopped today and my mother will be cooking dinner every afternoon."

He spun away from the stove to see Madelyn standing in the doorway. Dressed in denim shorts and a pink T-shirt, she could have been a teenager. Even the baby on her hip didn't make her look any older. Recognizing that nothing could make Madelyn look old enough for an affair with him should have stifled the immediate surge of attraction Ty felt for her. It didn't. Instead of her youth and enthusiasm making him feel old and battered, somehow looking at her made him feel younger.

Luckily, he knew better. "I didn't hire your mother."

"No, you didn't. But she's not helping you. She's helping me."

"I'm not paying her."

"She doesn't care. She's helping anyway."

"Why?"

"Because I bit off more than I can chew and family helps out when trouble strikes."

"I know what family does. I raised two brothers, remember?"

Madelyn looked at him oddly. "That's right. You have *two* brothers."

He sighed. There was that age difference again. She wasn't even old enough to remember his younger brother Cooper. "Not only have we talked about this before, but I would have thought you would have easily remembered since there are four bedrooms upstairs. One for my parents, and one each for three kids."

Madelyn gaped at him. "This was your family home?"

"Why does that surprise you?"

Madelyn sat on one of the kitchen chairs as if too shocked to stand, dropping the baby on her lap. "This explains a few things. Like why everybody thinks you're a scrooge."

"Keeping my parents' house makes me a scrooge?"

"You're a rich guy. You should have a mansion. Instead you live in a house you inherited." She glanced around, as if taking inventory. "You probably never even remodeled it."

"It didn't *need* to be remodeled and I don't *need* a mansion. This house is good enough."

"Whatever. But I'll need to know everything about

your second brother. I must have been too young to have met him when I lived here before."

Well, thanks for rubbing that in. "His name is Cooper. He graduated from college and struck out on his own. End of story."

Madelyn studied him for a few seconds, then she sighed. "If there's more to it than that, if you had a big fight, if your brother bad-mouthed you, I need to know what happened."

"My brother did not bad-mouth me. If anything my brother left so he *wouldn't* bad-mouth me." He squeezed his eyes shut. Damn. If she didn't get to him one way, she did another. "Stop poking your nose where it doesn't belong and do your job."

"My nose belongs anywhere I sense there's a problem that's hurting your reputation. If your brother's a problem, I need to know."

"My brother left town with a college education that gave him the opportunity to be as successful as Seth and I are."

"That's another thing. Seth is so darned withdrawn and cautious. One public show of support from you would probably turn him into Mr. Personality."

"He *was* Mr. Personality until he lost that contract I told you about on Saturday. I like him much better withdrawn and cautious. It doesn't cost me any money."

He turned and headed for the door. "I'm going back to the Bryant Building."

"Fine, but you should know that your constant running out on me, avoiding looking for a nanny, makes you look like even more of a scrooge."

He backpedaled until he was directly in front of her.

"Why do you think I'm going back to the office? So I can make some *private* calls. Some calls that won't be overheard, dissected, interpreted and spit back at me like ammunition. If nothing else, Ms. Gentry, you've shown me a few traits I definitely do not want in the next caregiver I allow in my home."

Chapter Five

Ty raced along the streets of Porter, so angry that he finally understood what the term spitting fire meant. He'd intended to lay down the law with Madelyn about her bringing the baby to the office, about pushing her agendas, about meddling in his business and instead she'd blindsided him. She had not only brought her parents into his home—again—without his knowledge, she'd also turned the tables until he was defending himself to her, not putting her on the defensive.

Unfortunately, he knew he wasn't at his best because his attraction to her distracted him. Worse, the attraction was the only thing he was just about certain she *wasn't* using, manipulating or twisting to get him to appear to be something he wasn't—*nice*—or to do things he didn't want to do—like hold Sabrina in the middle of a meeting. So he couldn't even order her to stop. Hell, he'd *tried* getting her to stop giving him those lovesick puppy looks on Friday night. By kissing her, he'd forced her to see, feel and taste exactly what she was getting into so she would know…

Both Ty's thoughts and his SUV screeched to a stop.

Well, darn her little hide. She was doing to him what he had done to her. She was forcing him to deal with the baby, to deal with the PR, to deal with his employees, by throwing him into those types of situations. It wasn't exactly the same as how and why he'd kissed her, but it was damned close. So close he might even have given her the idea!

But she was better at it than he was. She was so good he hadn't realized what she was doing. Worse, he'd walked right into her trap and behaved exactly as she needed him to behave. As if he were some kind of simpleton.

No, as if he were some kind of ogre. It appeared she had bought into everything his employees had told her in the days he had been out of the office for Scotty's funeral. But she wasn't changing the employees' impression of him. She was changing *him*.

He'd be damned.

He squelched the surge of disappointment that she thought he was as mean, as ornery, as unlikable as his employees believed. A personal relationship between them couldn't happen. And he liked being thought of as ornery. It gave him an edge with the employees. No one questioned any of his orders for fear he would yell. Which actually meant he rarely had to yell.

He also stomped down an unexpected surge of appreciation for both her cleverness and her ability to put her plans into action. Because *he* was the person she was hoodwinking, he couldn't applaud that.

He sat in the middle of Oak Avenue for only another thirty seconds before the driver of the car behind him honked his horn, indicating Ty should get going.

Yeah, he would get going all right. He would go straight home and put such a crimp in the plan of little Miss Public Relations that she'd never, *ever* try to bulldoze anyone again.

Madelyn was feeding Sabrina rice cereal when Ty returned. "What the heck?" she said, when she heard his SUV pull into the driveway close to the kitchen door.

She almost rose to glance out the window to be sure it was him, but he was in the kitchen before she got off her chair.

His penetrating onyx eyes pinned her and she felt a chill of foreboding run down her spine. She was in trouble. Deep trouble.

"I think you're going to need to teach me a few things about the baby."

Fearing a reprimand, or the prospect of being fired again, Madelyn wasn't expecting that request. "Really?"

"Yeah." He ran his finger along the bridge of his nose trying to appear casual, but Madelyn knew there was nothing casual about this guy. He did nothing without a reason. That was why she had had to trick him into looking like a good dad and a nice person. He would never choose to be either because both eroded his reputation as a scrooge, bully and tyrant.

"Did you call a nanny service and discover you were going to have to do night duty or something?"

"Nope. Didn't call yet. Not going to call until I can take care of Sabrina myself."

Terror skittered through Madelyn as she envisioned herself teaching him—and living here—until Sabrina graduated from college. "Are you kidding me?"

Obviously seeing her fear, he smiled. "No. I simply want to learn how to care for the baby."

"Great." Yeah, great. It didn't make a whit of sense that he'd changed his mind. She knew that undeniably meant he was up to something. She almost swallowed, but refused to show him any weakness. In fact, the best thing to do would be to meet his challenge head-on.

"Why don't we start with your feeding her the rest of her cereal?"

The baby pounded on the high chair as if signaling her approval.

He shrugged off his jacket. "Okay."

"You might want to change out of more than your coat."

"I'm already burning a pair of Armani pants. Another suit won't make any difference. I need to learn this."

The determination in his voice again confused Madelyn until she realized *that* was the deal. He'd figured out that the baby always threw him off balance and that using his confusion was how she guided him to do the things that would come naturally to him if he wasn't so busy being aloof, trying to convince everyone he didn't have a nice side. And having seen her strategy, he had resolved to take away her advantage.

Well, she'd see about that.

"Feeding a baby is a very simple thing."

Sabrina contradicted that by screeching and pounding her fist against the high chair tray, almost toppling the bowl.

Ty nodded. "First, I'd probably set the bowl on the

table," he observed, sounding as if he was approaching this the way he did a business problem and already coming up with better ways to do things.

"You could do that," Madelyn agreed calmly, not letting him gloat. "But having to turn back to the table to get bites will add time to the process and Sabrina's not going to like it."

"Really?"

"When she's hungry, she wants to eat. So leave the bowl on the tray, but watch it, and her." Madelyn smiled as if she'd told him something easy, when they both knew that watching Sabrina and the bowl would be far from simple. "Just get a little bite of cereal on the baby spoon and slide it into her mouth."

With the bowl on the tray, Ty did as instructed and Sabrina eagerly opened her mouth. Madelyn saw the determined expression in his eyes soften. But not with love for the baby. Nope. The expression in his eyes softened with relief. He was beating Madelyn and he was doing it deliberately.

Or so he thought.

"I'm glad you didn't call about the nanny," Madelyn said, going back to the strategy that had already worked so nicely for her. Confuse, disorient and conquer. "Because I realized something while you were gone."

"Really." He slid another spoonful of cereal into hungry Sabrina's mouth. This time his eyes sharpened. He'd gone from relief to victory in two spoonfuls.

"Yes. For the next few months the nanny may not mind sleeping in the same room with the baby on the same floor with her employer, but eventually she'll want more privacy." She glanced around the kitchen toward the laundry room, as if thinking through what he could do. "The only way she'll get real privacy is if you put her quarters downstairs, but that will be cramped. I think you're going to need to buy a new house."

"Something bigger," he ventured.

Well, now, that was too darned agreeable. "Yeah. Bigger."

"Sure, so that the nanny can have her own quarters."

Damn it! What was he doing? "Yeah."

"And while we're on the subject of houses," Ty said, spooning another bite into Sabrina's mouth. "I suppose I hadn't made myself clear before this, but I don't wish to have Captain Bunny and the Sarge roaming through my house at will."

"Captain Bunny and the Sarge?"

"Your parents. In case you haven't noticed, I like my privacy. I don't want strangers rooting through my things."

"My parents don't root through your things!"

"How do you know? You weren't here while they were stocking the house with groceries."

"Are you kidding me?"

He rose, growing angry now. "This is my home." He began walking to the kitchen doorway where Madelyn stood leaning against the frame. "I have a right to privacy."

She straightened away from the security of the door and squared her shoulders. "And I have a right to eat!"

"So go shopping yourself!" He took a step closer.

She took a deep breath that made her feel taller, stronger. This was it. Armageddon. She either won this fight or it was over. All of it. She would not be the wishy-washy employee who let him get away with not raising his own child just to maintain his scrooge image. She would stand up to him and teach him or she would leave. "When? I'm not even sleeping anymore!"

He took the final step that put him directly in front of her and forced her to look up at him. "You should have thought of that before you made the agreement."

Though her chin was tipped up in an unspoken testimonial to his superior height, she made sure her eyes told him she was conceding *nothing* and was a lot tougher than he thought.

"Ha! You should have considered your schedule before you agreed to 'do anything I said' for the baby and for the PR!"

"I've held up my end of the deal." Though she didn't think it possible he somehow got even closer.

"Not hardly." She raised the heat in her eyes a notch. "Every time I ask you to do something you have an excuse for why you can't."

"Legitimate reasons."

"Our agreement doesn't leave room for reasons. You said you would do *anything* I wanted for both the baby and the PR, yet all I get are excuses. You're the one who's letting me down." She paused, her eyes locked with his. "No. You're letting *the baby* down."

They stood nose to nose. Their gazes clashing. Both breathing heavily. Both out of steam.

With no more points to be made or defended, Madelyn suddenly noticed how masculine he was when he was out of control with the passion of his conviction. She didn't want to be attracted to him. He was too old for her and he wasn't the kind of man she always pictured herself getting involved with. But she couldn't deny that standing so close she could virtually feel his power. That strength was as attractive as his dark hair and eyes.

When he pulled his gaze away from hers, she relaxed somewhat, but he didn't step back as she expected he would. Instead, his gaze took a quick inventory of her body, and when she realized he was as attracted to her as she was to him, heat spiraled through her.

Determined to ignore the sexual electricity sizzling between them, she took the step back and shifted her attention to the fact that she was actually winning a battle with him. He wasn't arguing anymore because he couldn't argue. He seemed to finally see that not picking up his end of the responsibilities didn't hurt her, it hurt the baby.

Trying to get his mind off how soft Madelyn's skin looked, how plump her lips were and how easy it would be to kiss her again, Ty focused his attention on the fact that she was right. He wasn't merely Sabrina's "guardian." He was her *father*. He had to pay more attention to her.

He was suddenly glad Madelyn was bold enough to stand up to him, but he quickly amended that. She wasn't just bold enough to stand up to him. She out-and-out fought with him. Like an equal. That realization sent a thunderbolt of arousal through him. He looked at women as competent employees, friends, conquests, agreeable sex partners, but never his equal.

That was why the difference in their ages didn't deter his libido. Her age didn't matter because intellectually she was his equal.

He swallowed and watched Madelyn risk a quiet breath. One of them had to take another step back. And quickly.

Sabrina screeched noisily, then pounded her spoon against the high chair tray. Both he and Madelyn glanced over in time to see the baby grab the cereal bowl and heave it across the room. White mush splattered everywhere, including Ty's back.

Madelyn began to laugh. She laughed so long and hard, tears formed in her eyes. Ty stared at her. She was so different from anybody he'd ever met that he wasn't sure what to say or do. And not just about their work situation. He had to do something about the chemistry between them. Either stop it or enjoy it. Because he knew they would enjoy it. In fact, he was beginning to believe that if he let her get away without following through on their natural instincts, they might regret it for the rest of their lives.

"I think I need to change my shirt," he said, stepping back.

"Yeah," Madelyn said between giggles. "I'll take care of the baby."

"Then we need to talk."

"Uh-huh."

Ty left the room. He didn't know what he was going to say. All he knew for sure was that something had to change.

Madelyn turned from the counter when Ty returned to the kitchen ten minutes later. But wearing jeans and a T-shirt, looking relaxed and comfortable, he was incredibly attractive to her again. Worse, she now knew he found her attractive. He couldn't deny it because he hadn't been able to hide it. He couldn't even bluster his way out of it. Being as close and as passionately angry as he had been, he hadn't had his usual personal control and she'd seen the way he'd looked at her.

Still, their attraction was secondary to the baby. "I wiped the cereal off everything."

"So I see," he said, then glanced at Sabrina. "How do I get her out of the high chair?"

"There are levers on both sides of the tray. You squeeze them and the tray slides off. But don't take it the whole way off. Just open it far enough that you can pull her out."

"Okay," he said, and followed her instructions, creating a space through which he lifted the baby. "Hello, Sabrina," he said, tickling her chin. She giggled. "You really are an adorable kid."

Madelyn smiled. "She really is."

He drew a long breath. "And I understood what you were saying about my caring for her."

"It isn't that you have to care for her," Madelyn said cautiously, not wanting to make him think she was shirking her responsibilities. "You can hire someone to do the menial tasks. But she needs to spend time with you. When you come in the room, you should acknowledge her. When you leave, say goodbye. Kiss her goodnight. Give her ten minutes of playtime. Read her a story."

He smiled slightly. "And let someone else change diapers?"

"Sure."

"Good."

With their only neutral topic exhausted, the silence in the room became oppressive. Still, Madelyn didn't break it. Ty was the one who had said he wanted to talk. As long as they were discussing the baby, she could converse for hours. But she didn't have a clue what to say if he wanted to dissect their sexual attraction. If he asked her to sleep with him, she would probably consider it. But she also knew it would be wrong. At least, she suspected it would be wrong. He wasn't the kind of guy to settle down. He'd already told her he liked sophisticated women. She wasn't foolish enough to think she was the one woman who would change his entire life. And he'd already guessed she wanted to be married. If they made love, it would be a one-night stand, or an affair.

And that was the end of thinking about that! He was her boss. Even if she hadn't yet been hired full-time, she was working directly for him. Plus, she hoped to get the job as head of PR for Bryant Development. She couldn't have a one-night stand or an affair with him.

But with him standing three feet away, looking casual and comfortable, the thought of sleeping with him was tempting. So darned tempting!

Which was why they had to talk about this. They had to get it out in the open and agree to do whatever they had to do to ignore whatever it was that simmered between them.

Finally, Ty said, "So what do we do now?"

"Sabrina needs a bath, then a story, then another diaper change, then a bottle, then bed."

"Wow."

"Do you want to help with any of those?"

"I could do the story."

"You could do the story and the last bottle, actually. That way you could kiss her good-night while I showered and had a few minutes to myself."

"It's a deal."

Madelyn was acting strangely around him now, Ty noticed, when he slipped into the nursery to read to Sabrina. Her voice was husky when she explained her story choice. Her smile intimate when she handed him the book. In their last disagreement they'd crossed a line and he wasn't sure how to get them back on the right side.

As he read Sabrina a tale of a bunny's birthday, he heard the sound of Madelyn's shower and understood why she had insisted he needed to buy a new house. Because caring for a child was a twenty-four-hour-a-day job, he and Madelyn weren't simply sharing duties. They were living together. Hearing each other's showers. Exposed to each other's sleep-tousled hair and ready-for-bed yawns. They saw each other's most routine activities and nonetheless were sexually attracted. Then they went to bed knowing that the other slept beyond only a thin wall. And tonight that knowledge would keep them both awake.

But Madelyn couldn't leave and Ty couldn't have her leave yet, so they couldn't explore the sexual energy that constantly sizzled between them. That meant he had to get them back over that line again.

Madelyn returned to her bedroom wearing sweatpants and a big T-shirt, not pajamas and a robe as he had feared. Still, her nerves were clearly on edge, as if anticipating that any minute could be the minute he swept her off her feet. The funny part of it was that in the way she waited for it, she invited it.

"Here, I'll lay her in bed," Madelyn whispered, lifting Sabrina from his arms so he could rise from the rocker. "Then I'll leave while you tuck her in and kiss her good-night."

He nodded.

Madelyn laid the baby in the crib and Ty did as she had directed. He kissed the baby's forehead and pulled the fluffy blanket to her chin. He stared at her for a few seconds, wondering how one sixteen-pound bundle of noise could change his life so much.

He left the bedroom and found Madelyn in the family room. Standing in front of a row of DVDs, she appeared to be casually choosing something to watch but Ty could feel tense waves of expectation rolling off her. It tightened his nerves and brought urges to life that Ty wanted to act on. Nanny problems be damned.

Anita resurfaced in his memory, but not because Madelyn and Anita looked or acted alike. Madelyn and Anita were total opposites. Anita was a short brunette with big brown eyes and curly hair. Madelyn was tall, slender, sleek, graceful.

But the real difference between them, and probably what attracted him to Madelyn now, was Madelyn's maturity. Still Ty wasn't fooled. Mature or not, Madelyn couldn't handle working with him after their affair ended. Anybody would have trouble having an ex-lover for a boss. He also had to consider sexual harassment potential. But even if—by some miracle—things somehow worked out between them, he never wanted to settle down. Girlfriends were a drain on his time. They were a security risk. They had friends. They talked at cocktail parties. Wanted to have lunch in the middle of the week. Expected vacations. Wanted to talk at dinner.

As pretty as Madelyn was, as interesting as she was, she would take up his time, talk about his life in public, air his dirty laundry, get involved with his family issues, tell him how to raise Sabrina....

Did he need any more reasons than those to walk away?

But he didn't have time to turn and run before Madelyn faced him. Her warm green eyes drew him in from across the room. Her pretty smile tempted him.

Without any effort at all he remembered kissing her. He remembered her taste, the softness of her lips, and his blood pulsed hard through his veins. He wondered what she would be like in bed and knew her body would be soft and responsive. She would be passionate. But making love with her would be more than something physical.

He gritted his teeth in frustration, wondering what the hell it was about this woman that affected him so powerfully. She wasn't superwoman. She didn't hold the answers to the universe. She was a kid who knew how to help him with the baby that had been dumped into his lap. His cousin had died, he'd unceremoniously become a father and he was about to face the press—something he'd avoided for fifteen years. His life had been tossed up in the air and was coming down in disjointed pieces. He shouldn't be thinking about sex right now.

For God's sake, the very woman tempting him was the one who was messing up his life!

No matter how much he tried to believe otherwise, his attraction to Madelyn was nothing but a physical thing. Once he got a nanny, he could fly to New York and visit a female friend and anything he felt for his little PR pal, who was far too young for him anyway, would be gone.

"I'm going to my study."

"Oh. I thought you wanted to talk."

Her eyes were soft, luminous, as if he'd hurt her. Her smile faltered. An odd tightening began in Ty's chest. He knew he was the cause of the confusion he saw on her face. But that was the very reason he couldn't change his mind. In the end, he would hurt her and, contrary to popular belief, he never deliberately hurt anyone.

"I changed my mind."

He sighed heavily and raked his hand through his hair. "Just go to bed and get some rest while the kid is sleeping, would you?"

Chapter Six

Madelyn bounced out of bed the next morning energized by her lingering fury over what had happened the night before between her and Ty. He could no longer pretend he wasn't attracted to her. She'd seen the desire that flared in his eyes when they'd confronted each other. Yet after telling her they needed to talk, making her believe they would approach this attraction like two adults—and that he might even kiss her again—he came into the living room and shipped her to her room as if she were a child.

Carefully lifting Sabrina out of her crib, cooing a good-morning at the happy baby, Madelyn reluctantly admitted to herself that she hadn't reacted well. Ty had made her so angry that she actually did as he'd asked. But that was because he behaved as if this whole attraction mess was her fault, as if she *wanted* to be attracted to him.

Ha! It killed her to have physical responses to him because he really wasn't her type. Though gorgeous, and now becoming involved with the baby, he was still ill-tempered, selfish and single-minded. The words *share* and *compromise* were not in his vocabulary—evidenced by the fact that he knew they needed to talk about their attraction, but he'd apparently decided to handle it his own way and banished her to her room.

Madelyn paused her thoughts as she held giggling Sabrina over the baby bathtub. She recognized Ty had shipped her out because he didn't want to talk about their attraction. But what if the way he had decided to deal with it was to stay away from her completely? What if he ordered her not to come to the office?

No. He wouldn't do that. He knew she had a lot of work to do before the *Wall Street Journal* reporter arrived. He was too pragmatic to prevent her from doing her job.

When Sabrina was dressed, Madelyn carried her to the kitchen and slid her into the high chair, then went to the cupboard in search of ingredients for the baby's cereal. As Madelyn reached for a bowl, Ty dashed in. Looking handsome in a dark suit with a white shirt and red tie, he didn't pause or even stop for coffee. He simply shot toward the back door barking orders.

"I think it's time you took inventory of the diaper bags and bought whatever Sabrina needs that we don't have. Pajamas, rattles, teddy bears. Buy whatever Pete didn't pack. I put two hundred dollars on my desk, if you need more, there's a credit card. I also left the number for my gardener. Call him and tell him to get the hell over here and cut my grass."

Without waiting for an answer Ty slammed the door behind him and Madelyn stood staring at it. He really was keeping her home because he couldn't handle their attraction.

She stopped her thoughts. It didn't matter why he gave her orders that kept her out of the office. She had work to do beyond being Sabrina's nanny and she intended to do it.

"Sorry," she said, her voice low even though she knew he was in the SUV by now and couldn't hear anything she said. "But I have to come to the office today. If I don't get my PR strategies up and running, the employees won't be ready when the *Wall Street Journal* reporter gets here. Don't worry though. My mother will do the shopping. And my dad will call your gardener. I'll see you at the office."

There. If he had been playing high-handed boss, she had just balanced the scales. If he wasn't being high-handed, but genuinely wanted Sabrina to have everything she needed, then Madelyn had simply taken care of his tasks differently than how he'd suggested. She might have agreed to be Sabrina's nanny, but she also had work to do. And she wasn't going to let *his* fear of their chemistry prevent her from doing it.

An hour later, with her parents assigned their respective chores and Sabrina tucked in the back seat of Madelyn's car, Ty's temporary nanny drove to work. But when she pulled into a parking space, her bravado from the kitchen began to fail her. As Sabrina cooed behind her, Madelyn stared at the huge brown brick Bryant Building, a symbol of how powerful Ty was, took a long breath and gave herself a minute to muster her courage.

But all she could think of were reasons she should *not* enter that building. The most relevant was that she and Ty had gotten into the fight that sent their sexual chemistry off the charts because he had been angry about the way she had manipulated him. Though she wasn't precisely manipulating him this morning, she wasn't following his orders. When she showed up in her office with Sabrina, Ty would probably hit the roof. That wouldn't be good for the new image she was working to create for him.

Madelyn took a cleansing breath, reminding herself that Ty hadn't said she *couldn't* come into the office or that she *couldn't* bring Sabrina. He had said to take inventory and call the gardener. And both of those errands were being done. So, technically, she wasn't disobeying him and if he saw her and he looked like he was about to explode, she would explain that to him. Everything would be okay.

She took another deep breath and grabbed the handle of her car door. "Come on, Sabrina."

She entered the lobby, carrying Sabrina on one arm and the jumbo diaper bag on the other.

"Hello, Madelyn! Hello, Miss Sabrina!" Ginny greeted them.

"Good morning, Ginny," Madelyn said, then turned to the baby. "Say hello, Sabrina."

Sabrina screeched. Madelyn kissed her cheek. "Isn't she precious?"

Ginny sighed. "Absolutely."

"She just melts Ty's heart," Madelyn said, keeping up the impression that Ty was a normal person by subtly slipping tidbits of his life with Sabrina into everyday conversation.

Ginny snorted a laugh. "Maybe. But having a baby hasn't improved his disposition at work. He came in this morning looking like a bear with a thorn in his paw."

Madelyn reveled in perverse satisfaction that he wasn't any happier than she was until she remembered she could very well be on the wrong side of his dark mood in only a few minutes.

"I think he's a little out of sorts today because he didn't take any time this morning with Sabrina," she told Ginny as she walked to the elevator. The rosy picture she painted of Ty with Sabrina wasn't really a lie. Since she didn't know—well, wasn't absolutely positive of the reason for Ty's bad humor—it wasn't such a farfetched guess that his mood stemmed from missing that morning's interaction with the baby. Not only was he getting better at caring for Sabrina, but he had made a commitment to be a better parent. If there was one thing she knew about Ty he kept his commitments.

"See you at lunch," Madelyn said as the elevator bell rang and the door opened. She entered and pressed the button for her floor. After the short ride, she took another fortifying breath, stepped into the corridor and walked down the path made by two rows of cubicles on her way to her office.

As she passed each individual workstation, the occupant rose, peered over the five-foot divider and cooed at the baby. Sabrina ate it up. Laughing, singing, cooing back. Madelyn squared her shoulders and stood taller. Whether Ty knew it or not, the baby was doing a bang-up job of getting his employees to see him as being more human, and that opened the door for Madelyn to talk about his good points—even if she did stretch the truth a bit. If he dared argue with her about coming to work, she might just sock him.

By the time Madelyn reached her office, the energy and courage she'd failed to muster in the car flowed abundantly through her veins.

"Can I come in?"

Madelyn set Sabrina in the play yard that she'd set up by her desk the first day she brought Sabrina to work, and turned to see Seth standing in her doorway. Dressed in a pair of khaki trousers with a dark brown jacket that brought out the yellow in his sandy hair, Seth was Ty's polar opposite. Not that he wasn't good-looking. He was every bit as attractive as his older brother, but in a boy-next-door kind of way. Ty was handsome in a sexy, deliciously masculine kind of way….

Taking a quick breath, Madelyn reprimanded herself for thinking those thoughts about a man who was all wrong for her, and smiled at Seth.

"Of course, you can come in! What can I do for you?"

He closed the door. "I heard you walking down the hall with the baby and wanted to have a minute with her."

"That's a great idea!" Madelyn said, pulling Sabrina out of the play yard so she could hand the little girl to Seth.

But Seth waved his hands in refusal and stepped back. "I'm not sure what to do."

Madelyn nudged the baby toward him again. "Just take her."

He hesitated. "Okay," he said, then awkwardly wrapped his hands around Sabrina's waist. He laughed. "She's so…smooshy."

"That's her diaper. It makes her feel very soft and pliable."

"Hey, Sabrina," Seth said, nuzzling his nose under her chin.

Sabrina stared at him, then hooked her fingers around a lock of his pale hair, yanking on it.

"Ouch," Seth singsonged, not in any real pain.

Madelyn beamed. "See how you did that? That's the perfect reaction."

Seth glanced at Madelyn. "It is?"

"Sure, you let Sabrina know that what she was doing wasn't right, but you weren't mean about it. You sort of made it a game."

Seth virtually glowed from the praise. "Really?"

"You're a natural."

Sabrina playfully patted Seth's cheek. "Thanks. I know what it's like not to have parents. This kid is going to feel alone and different. So, I intend to play a part in her life."

"That's very sweet," Madelyn said, wondering how someone Ty raised could be so thoughtful, and also remembering that Ty and Seth had another brother. One who had run away. One who might not be as sweet as Seth, but who could actually be more like Ty. And one whose story might poke a big ugly hole in Madelyn's carefully orchestrated PR plan.

Since Ty wasn't forthcoming with information, she strolled behind her desk, flipped the calendar page to the appropriate day and, as if it were of little consequence, casually said, "I imagine it was very difficult being orphaned. Especially when raised through most of your teen years by such a high-profile older brother."

Seth peered around Sabrina at Madelyn. "Ty wasn't always a big shot."

"That's right. The first five years that you guys were on your own he nearly went bankrupt every year."

"It wasn't because he didn't try."

"Oh, believe me, I'm sure he tried."

"He was great." Seth smiled at the memory. "Tough as nails and so freaking determined to succeed that he didn't let anybody stand in his way."

Madelyn banished the image of a young, sexy Ty taking on the world by forcing herself to focus on the conversation with Seth. Though she had to admit that remembering how he'd struggled as a young man, particularly since he was also supporting two brothers at the time, did tweak her conscience, making her feel she should consider how hard his life had been before she criticized him for taking the easy way out in dealing with their attraction. "That's interesting."

"Yeah, and it's old news to you. You have access to every file in the building so I know you know all this. What are you fishing for?"

Madelyn winced and decided to come clean. "Seth, I need to know what I'm going to be facing if the reporter uncovers information about Cooper leaving town. Ty won't talk about it, so I'm guessing it's not something good. If you believe the reason Cooper left needs to remain a secret, or if you know Ty wants it to remain a secret, just explain enough of it to me that I can create an answer that spins the situation into something acceptable if the reporter asks about it."

Sabrina grabbed Seth's ear as he said, "The real bottom line was that Ty never believed Cooper respected him. But in the end it was Ty who didn't respect Cooper. And that's why Cooper left. He didn't want to work for someone who didn't respect him. Brother or not."

Well, that didn't sound too bad. Still, she had to be sure. "So there was no fight? Nothing I have to spin?"

"Oh, there was a fight. A big fight. But no one saw it or heard about it except me and that was only because I was upstairs. Ty certainly never talked about it in public and Cooper left before he could."

Madelyn tapped her fingers on her desk blotter. Seth's answer explained Ty's comment that Cooper left town so he wouldn't bad-mouth his older brother. "So if the reporter asks about Cooper, what would you say to make his leaving seem reasonable?"

Seth drew a quick breath. "I would say he got his degree and two years experience and left to find a job in another town. Because that was how the timing went."

"What if the reporter knows you guys haven't had contact in almost a decade?"

Seth shrugged. "We're all very busy, Madelyn."

Madelyn nodded. "Okay, I can take that and craft an acceptable statement for Ty."

"I don't think you have to," Seth said as he passed the baby back to Madelyn. "Ty's been spinning this story for years. If the topic comes up, he'll handle it beautifully."

She took the little girl and kissed her cheek. "So, you think I should trust him?"

"Yes."

When Madelyn looked up, Seth was smiling at her.

"You're very good with her."

"Thanks. I've had plenty of practice with babies because I have eight nieces and nephews."

Seth laughed. "Eight nieces and nephews! Wow," he

said, but his smile faded. "You know, after all this talk about Cooper I just realized he's been gone so long, he could be married. *I* could have a niece or nephew."

"Or several," Madelyn agreed.

Seth toyed with the stapler on her desk. "I tried to find him, you know."

"Cooper?" Madelyn glanced over at him. "Really? Did Ty know?"

Seth shrugged. "I doubt it. I had a private investigator looking. I wasn't doing the legwork myself, and the P.I. only poked around for a few weeks before I told him to stop. But he hadn't gotten anywhere anyway, so I'm not sure we'd ever actually find Cooper, even if we looked for years."

"Why did you tell your P.I. to stop?"

Seth swallowed, then turned away, and Madelyn's breath caught. All this time she was worried about Cooper being the loose cannon when the real problem might be right under her nose. With Seth behaving so oddly she had to wonder if he didn't have a secret, too. "No reason to keep looking."

"Seth, is there something you want to tell me?"

"No."

"Really? Because it seems like something is wrong."

"I'm fine."

"You don't look fine."

Seth laughed. "Madelyn, there's nothing about my past that's going to pop up and hurt my brother. Trust me. Anything I did that might potentially be embarrassing—and that's all it would be is embarrassing—has been so tidily buried by real pros that you don't need to worry about it."

After he was gone, Madelyn sat Sabrina in the play

yard, then stared at her closed office door with her arms crossed over her chest. She had been at Bryant Development long enough, and had spent enough time interacting with Seth that if there had been a real problem Seth would have told her. She cringed for a minute over his statement that his situation had been "buried by real pros" but kept coming back to his assertion that his past was only "embarrassing" and she could handle embarrassing.

Unfortunately, talking with Seth hadn't sufficiently eased her mind about Cooper, and she decided she was done mollycoddling Ty. Seth's problem might only be embarrassing, but it caused him to be moody and emotional, and Madelyn couldn't risk him leaking something about the story of Ty's fight with Cooper that could potentially come back to haunt them. So, tonight, whether Ty liked it or not, he was telling her the entire story.

Not wanting to rile Ty before they had the discussion about Cooper, Madelyn only stayed at the office until noon. When she opened the door to the kitchen, she found a note from her mother sitting on the table.

She slid Sabrina into the high chair and slipped out of her pink pumps as she read the missive, which told her about a slow-roasting chicken that was in the oven.

"It's too bad you can't eat this," she told the baby who gurgled her response. "My mother makes the best stuffed chicken."

"Lucky for us."

At the sound of Ty's voice, Madelyn spun around. "What are you doing here?"

"I saw you brought the baby to work again, so I came

home to call nannies. Almost shot Captain Bunny as an intruder."

Madelyn dropped her head to her head. "Oh, no!"

Ty brushed off her concern. "Don't worry. We handled it. Your mother is actually a very nice person."

Madelyn breathed a sigh of relief. "I take it she didn't have my dad with her."

"No. Thank God. The Sarge must have stayed home." He walked to the high chair and looked down at Sabrina, as if not sure what to do.

"Pick her up. Give her a hug. Kiss her cheek."

Ty took a deep breath.

"Ty, you have to kiss her, hug her, touch her. You and Seth are her only family. If you don't show her affection, no one will."

Ty nodded, then raised the baby from the seat and into his arms. "Hey, kid."

Looking into Ty's face, Sabrina twisted her head as if examining him.

"She's growing accustomed to you."

"At least it doesn't seem like she misses her *M-O-M* anymore."

Madelyn laughed at the way he spelled rather than said mom, but her expression quickly sobered. "That isn't just lucky for us. It's kind of lucky for Sabrina, too."

"Yeah," Ty said, then rubbed his nose against Sabrina's cheek. "It's sad, though."

"Yes, it is," Madelyn agreed. Seeing her perfect opportunity to ask him about Cooper, she added, "You and Seth and your brother Cooper know firsthand how hard it is to lose parents."

Ty stiffened. "We're fine."

Right. Madelyn disagreed with that, but she also saw that having Ty defensive was ruining his time with Sabrina. So she changed the subject, knowing she could bring this up later. "Tell me what happened with the nannies."

"I start interviewing tomorrow."

"Tomorrow?"

"Don't pack your bags yet. I'll probably have to do second interviews then once I choose somebody, it will take at least a week to do a background search."

A strange whirlwind of conflicting emotions swirled through Madelyn as she stared at Ty. With the sleeves of his white shirt rolled to the elbows and his tie loosened as he very sweetly nuzzled Sabrina, he was the most adorable, sexy man on the face of the earth. But she didn't like her attraction to him. Heck, she just plain didn't like *him* sometimes. On the other hand, she wasn't so stupid that she didn't see that Ty's employees believed her when she made observations about his private life because everyone knew she was living in his house, getting the inside scoop, seeing him with the baby. She didn't merely appreciate that edge. She needed it.

But even if her heart caught at the thought of leaving Ty, she couldn't stay here forever. Having any kind of feelings for him was foolish. His difficult life might justify his bad disposition, but that didn't make it any easier to live with. She didn't want to get involved with a grouch.

"Did she have a nap this morning?"

Madelyn glanced over at Ty, surprised that he was beginning to think ahead about Sabrina's needs. In two days he had gone from ignoring his baby to considering her comfort. If Madeline didn't so desperately want to stay here for her PR purposes, Ty's rapid signs of improvement with the baby would be confirmation that it was time to go. But she did need to stay here for the PR. At least until the *Wall Street Journal* reporter was gone.

"Yes. She napped this morning in the play yard in my office. She slept right through two meetings."

Ty shifted the baby to his right arm and peered at Madelyn, giving her such a confused look that she frowned.

"What?"

"I'm puzzled about whom you meet with."

He really had no clue about how public relations worked. "Your employees," she said in an attempt to enlighten him about her job. "Department heads mostly. I need to gauge how your employees will respond to the reporter about you and your company. That way I can steer him to the appropriate people."

Ty said, "I see."

"And you should speak kindly about *them* when the reporter asks *you* questions about the people who work for you."

Ty laughed. "Really? I have to say nice things about a bunch of people who hate me?"

"You don't have to say nice things to them, but it won't be a lie for you to say you think they're hardworking, honest people."

Tickling Sabrina, Ty didn't reply.

Madelyn's instincts perked up. "You do think they're honest, hardworking people, don't you?"

Ty shook his head. "Yes, but for the past fifteen years

they've been allowed to bad-mouth me—even though I've kept most of them employed. And I…" He sighed. "Never mind. I see what you mean and I'll say what you need me to say. Though it might give an interesting slant to the article if I told the truth and admitted their perpetual dislike makes it very easy for me to make tough choices." With that he walked to the kitchen door, Sabrina still on his arm. "I'm taking her into the family room to play for a few minutes. This will be our quality time for the day."

He left and an odd thought tiptoed into Madelyn's brain. He had a point. A very interesting point. He *had* employed virtually everyone in this town and no one appreciated it. Smart employees would have erected a statue in his honor, or at the very least made him man of the year. These employees went out of their way to persecute him.

Of course, he invited it. And now she realized why. His horrible reputation clearly kept his employees in line and made difficult decisions much easier to make. Everyone knew he was hard and cold, so no one disobeyed him. No one confronted him. No one challenged him. His word was law. His reputation allowed him to run the company the way he wanted to run it—without interference, without a boatload of questions, without having to explain himself—so he let his employees fear him to their hearts' content.

But living with him gave her a different view of his life and things didn't add up the way they did when she just looked at the surface. Ty supported nearly everyone in town. He had raised a very thoughtful brother in Seth. And he'd taken in an orphaned cousin. True, he was reluctant at first, but he had stepped in and was doing his duty with love and affection for Sabrina. Yet, his employees, the very people who counted on him for their paychecks, treated him abysmally, as if they didn't see the good he did.

Because they probably didn't see the good he did, or not enough of the good he did.

Madelyn suddenly got it. *This* was why Ty worked so hard to keep everyone out of his personal life. In two short weeks of living with him, seeing the quiet decisions and private choices, she was coming to the conclusion everybody else missed. Deep down inside, Tyrant Ty was a nice guy.

But he couldn't let anybody know that. If he got too chummy with his employees then he might not be able to make the hard choices he felt he needed to keep his company successful—and to continue employing the very people who disliked him.

So he never let anybody get close to him. But Madelyn was close. Albeit accidentally. That was why her feelings for him were so odd, unmanageable and sometimes even insane. She liked the side of him that no one else knew existed. But if she tried to tell anybody in this town there was another side to Tyrant Ty, a good side, no one would believe her.

That night Ty *volunteered* to learn how to bathe Sabrina. Madelyn explained the football hold that allowed the baby to be dipped in the water, while held securely on his arm. She showed him how to wash her gently with the baby products her mom had picked up. Then she taught him how to wrap Sabrina in her yellow terry-cloth robe and had him carry her to the changing table.

"Special soap, special shampoo, special ways to hold her. God, I'm glad my brothers were older when I inherited them."

"They might have been older but I'm sure they came with their own problems."

Ty sighed. "Ms. Gentry, you are not supposed to agree with me."

"Yeah, well," Madelyn said, rummaging through the drawer for an undershirt and sleepers. "I guess I'm just not in the mood to spar."

"Too bad."

The day before she would have guessed he thought it "too bad" that she didn't feel like bantering because he enjoyed the fight. Tonight she knew he was annoying her on purpose. Not because he wanted to protect them from another kiss, but because he was enforcing the idea that his life was easier when his employees disliked him.

She drew a quick breath. "Yeah, too bad," she said watching Ty towel dry the baby. "Look, I know you have work to do so I'll read to her and feed her her last bottle."

"I'm fine."

"I know. But technically I'm supposed to be doing this. It's good that you're learning, but when you hire a nanny she will do all these routine tasks."

Holding Sabrina on the changing table, he studied Madelyn. "You're not getting soft on me, are you?"

She wasn't getting soft, Madelyn thought as she motioned Ty aside so she could begin dressing the baby, but she was finally seeing the light. When she took her analysis of Ty Bryant to its logical conclusion she realized he had sacrificed having friendships, relationships, even the ability to take a walk down Main Street, because he believed having everyone dislike him was a small price to pay to be able to keep everyone employed.

Still, he would hate it if he knew she had begun to figure all this out. "No, I'm not getting soft."

"Good."

Madelyn said nothing as she returned her attention to dressing the baby.

Ty stared at her. Something wasn't right. Madelyn should either be applauding his efforts, acting like a cheerleader, or pushing him to change so he could give a good interview to the *Wall Street Journal* reporter. Yet she remained quiet.

"Who did you talk to today?"

"Aaron Ringwald in accounting. Megan Fontain in marketing."

He tried to think of something nice either of those employees might have said that would cause Madelyn to give up her mission to reform him and couldn't. He'd made Megan cry twice the month before. Aaron had been passed over for a promotion. If anything, talking to them should have increased her determination to change him.

Madelyn rolled Sabrina into a one-piece sleeper and Ty felt a tug on his heart. In a little over a week, he had grown to really like the little girl. He liked the way she smelled, the way she felt, even the sound of her voice. So if the tug on his heart trickled over into feelings for the baby's caregiver, he wasn't surprised. Now that he knew everything that went into baby care, he appreciated Madelyn's help. He even understood her reluctance to get involved.

That was why he counted on Madelyn disliking him. Why he barked orders and continued to treat her as a servant instead of a friend. They had to be adversaries. It was the easiest way to keep them both in line. And if she suddenly got quiet or quit defending herself, their attraction was likely to spring up again.

"I want to see you in my study when she's asleep." He would get to the bottom of whatever nice thing she'd thought he'd done and he would get her hating him again if it killed him.

Madelyn showed up in his study door about ten minutes later. Ty tossed his pencil to his desk blotter. "Baby asleep?"

She nodded.

He sighed. "Come in. Let's get this discussion over with. What did you hear today or figure out that has you acting so strangely?"

For a minute, Ty thought she wasn't going to tell him, but she sighed and said, "That you're a nice guy."

He laughed. This would be easy to counter. "Who told you that?"

"No one. I figured it out for myself. You raised your brothers, then when they were grown you shifted your focus to taking care of the town by making sure your company stayed successful."

"Not hardly. I built this company so I would be rich."

"That might be part of it, but you're proud that you employ almost everybody in town."

"Madelyn, I fire people. I yell at people. I can make vice presidents cry and not have a single regret."

"You have no qualms about pushing people because the company you're running supports them. *You* even said having your employees dislike you makes it easy for you to make tough decisions. It's pretty clear to me you're giving up friends and even a comfortable place in the community so you can ensure most of the people in this town have a job."

He dropped his head to his hands and wearily ran his palms down his face. "Oh, lord."

"Why won't you let me leak a little bit of this to your employees?"

"Leak what? That I raised my brothers? They know that."

"They also know that you took in Sabrina when there was no one else to raise her. But there's more to you than family responsibility. You have a huge sense of responsibility to this town. Such a sense of responsibility that you're willing to sacrifice your own personal life to make sure your company runs smoothly."

He stared at her incredulously. She honestly believed this crap she was telling him.

She drew another huge breath. "You might be gruff, Ty, but deep down you're a nice guy."

"Not even on a good day!" Angry now, he walked around the side of his desk and stood directly in front of her. "I told you in our first meeting that I had worked fifteen years to get this reputation and if you start spreading this manure you're going to screw it up."

"See! You just proved my argument. You *use* this

reputation! But I think you've taken the grouch thing too far. Or maybe it's gone on too long. You don't have to be mean anymore to get your employees to work hard."

"Oh, really, Miss Smarty Pants. And how many companies do you successfully run?"

"You know what I'm saying."

He stepped closer. She didn't as much as move a muscle. If he was out to intimidate her, it was clear that she was every bit as determined to prove he couldn't. And that could very well be true. She might be the only person on the face of the earth who didn't fear him.

Suddenly he knew that was the problem but he also knew the solution.

He ran his fingers along her cheek, gently, tentatively, ignoring the tornado of arousal that spun through him when he realized how soft her skin was and when he saw the way her eyes darkened from a simple touch. Just as she considered it her mission to get his employees to speak kindly of him, he had an equally important mission to keep their respect. If the only way to keep her in line was to…

He bent his head and kissed her. The arousal that had begun with touching her cheek turned into a full-scale attack on his senses. The scent of her perfume combined with the taste of her mouth and the feeling of her lips pressed against his. The sensations of all three flooded through him, sending all his blood to one part of his body. His response was quick and instinctive. He fanned his fingers through her hair and plunged his tongue into her mouth, forgetting this kiss had a purpose. She was soft and warm and sweet and tempting. So tempting. Why did she have to be so tempting?

When he pulled away, she blinked up at him. Her green eyes were cloudy with desire. Her lips were moist and dewy from his kiss. He knew exactly what she was feeling because he was feeling it, too. But it was wrong. She was young. He was old. She thought the world was good. He knew it wasn't.

Though he was internally shaking with need, outwardly he remained calm. "If you really think I'm nice… If you really think I'm totally different personally than I am professionally…have sex with me tonight and see how I treat you in the morning."

With arousal still wreaking havoc on his nervous system and need pounding in his veins, Ty half prayed she would accept his invitation, if only to call his bluff, so he could feel the thrill of her acknowledging she wanted him, too.

Fortunately, he used the other half of his prayer to hope that if she called his bluff, he'd have the strength to refuse her.

Clearly debating, she stared at him. Ty felt his resolve weakening, as his mind formed images of what would happen if she agreed to go to his bed. With their chemistry, they would spontaneously combust and she knew it. It would be the best sex of both of their lives. And she knew that, too. What she was debating really was how he would treat her in the morning.

That she didn't know. So, that was what he had to use.

"Come on. You threw out the theory that I'm nice. Prove you really think that. Sleep with me tonight."

She took a pace back and Ty knew he had his answer. He felt a sharp jab of insult from the rejection, but re-

minding himself that he needed her to reject him, he ignored it and shook his head.

"I didn't think so." Turning to walk back to his desk,
he said, "Good night, Ms. Gentry."

Chapter Seven

The next morning Madelyn arrived at Bryant Development late for Ty's regularly scheduled meeting with his department heads. When she got off the elevator, she said good morning to Joni, then took a quick breath, straightened her shoulders and walked into the conference room.

"Ms. Gentry, I see you've decided to join us. Even though you're—" he glanced at his watch "—thirty minutes late."

Head high and spine ramrod straight, Madelyn took a seat at the far end of the long table. "I dropped Sabrina off at my parents' this morning."

"Really? What a novel idea to have a third party watch the baby rather than bring her to work."

Madelyn opened her notebook, glad he was behaving like a moron. She'd actually mourned her decision not to sleep with him the night before. Not because she wanted to prove she thought he was a good person, but because the fire burning through her veins every time they touched was unlike anything she'd ever felt.

Until he spoke. Because when he spoke, his true colors came out. He was probably the most self-absorbed, cold, emotionless man she'd ever met. If he had given her one word of tenderness or romance the night before, she would have melted. Instead, he'd propositioned her as if sex were nothing but a way to prove a point, insulting her to the tips of her toes. Yet in a way, that was lucky. His view of making love proved that she had been wrong about him. There wasn't a nice guy inside Ty. He was a one-dimensional, selfish, success-at-any-cost jerk. Madelyn kept giving him the benefit of the doubt because the good things he did confused her into thinking he had a heart. But he didn't. His sense of responsibility forced him to raise his brothers, provide a home for his cousin's child and create good jobs for the townspeople. He was responsible. He wasn't *nice.*

Still, as she watched him conduct his meeting, she couldn't stop the sexual awareness that snaked through her. He lifted his arm to point at a number on the overhead screen, opening his black jacket and exposing his white shirt, and she remembered there was a fabulous male form beneath because she'd seen him in jeans and T-shirts. She'd tasted the sureness of his kiss, the experience of it. Even without making love to this man, she felt sure he knew a million ways to pleasure a woman, and if they ever did succumb to their passion, the explosion would be surreal. The experience would be surreal.

She stopped that thought. Sex without emotion was

only sex and she shouldn't even be thinking about it. But she *was* curious. Damn curious. Still, she couldn't sleep with someone just for the fun of it. Especially not someone totally devoid of emotion. She had been brought up to want relationships with *good* men. Actually, having been taught to look for a morally upright man might explain why she kept theorizing that Ty Bryant had a good side. She was searching for a way to make her fantasy of sleeping with him legitimate.

But she now had solid confirmation that he wasn't a nice man and she also knew the best way to keep her sanity would be to quit initiating personal discussions with him. No more conversation. No more benefit of the doubt. No more temptation.

That night she implemented her decision to speak only when spoken to and then only about the appropriate topics, and to her complete horror it hurt when Ty seemed very, very happy with her new course of action. For two long days they hardly spoke, then at dinner the third day—completely out of the blue—Ty said, "Your mother is a very good cook."

"Thanks."

"But she doesn't have to do this, you know. From the way we nearly starved the first weekend, I got the message that my lifestyle had to change a bit. I can't go out for breakfast, lunch and dinner anymore, so I need to make accommodations. Breakfast I can get on the run. Lunch is usually taken care of at work. But I was thinking about calling Louie's and asking the owner to send over two dinners every night, so we don't have to impose on your mother."

Madelyn resisted the urge to smile at him. She wasn't sure if it was pragmatism that had him thinking about meals, or an unwillingness to take advantage of her mother's good nature, but either way his plan was unexpectedly considerate.

Still, there was no point in smiling. Instead, she politely said, "You'll probably have to do that when I leave, but for now my mother's very happy to send us dinner."

"Okay, then ask her to write up a bill and I'll…"

"Ty!" Madelyn protested, forgetting she wasn't supposed to be getting personal with him. "This is my mother! She likes doing this. Besides, there's nothing to bill. You're buying the groceries. She's donating her time, but she enjoys it."

He took a quick breath. "Then I want you to tell your parents to feel free to watch Sabrina here if it would make cooking easier."

Madelyn gaped at him. "You want them to watch Sabrina here?"

"Yes."

"In your house?"

"Yes."

"My dad, too?"

He grimaced, but recovered quickly. "Yes. I'm fine with the Sarge trooping through my backyard. Heck, if he wants, he can take a look at the flower bed and see if there's anything he wants to plant there."

Madelyn stared at Ty, but he went back to eating his dinner, Sabrina on his lap, as if nothing had happened. But *everything* had happened. He'd made a concession! Without her prodding him he had offered a kindness.

And it had nothing to do with responsibility. Somebody was doing something nice for him, so he did something nice in return.

She wasn't wrong! Inside Ty was a good man! She knew he kept that knowledge hidden because he thought being mean got him respect, but with a reporter about to descend on them and her entire public relations reputation on the line, she wasn't going to let him behave like a scrooge anymore.

She wanted that nice guy out and walking around the streets of Porter. And she knew exactly how to get him out and keep him out.

She waited until Friday when the baby was in bed and Ty was in his study, engrossed in reading something he'd brought home from work, before she sprung her trap.

"I'm ready to sleep with you now."

He peered up from the thick document. "I thought we'd been over this."

"We had, but I wasn't prepared for your offer. Today I'm prepared."

He leaned back in his chair. His eyes raked over her, but when he returned his gaze to her face, his expression was shuttered. Any emotion he was feeling was hidden. "Really?"

She wouldn't let herself shake or quake or lose heart. Too much was at stake here. "Yeah. See…" She drew a quick breath. "The point is, I think you're a great guy."

He snorted a laugh, but Madelyn kept talking.

"And you deserve a much better life than what you have…"

"A much better life?" He gaped at her. "I'm rich.

Nearly everybody in town works for me. And as long as I keep you in line, they all still respect me."

"Yes, they respect you, but you don't have friends."

"And you think I need friends."

"Everybody needs friends. But more than that, you need companionship."

He shifted in his tall-backed office chair and tossed his pencil on top of his document. "Really? And you think *you're* that companion."

This was the tough part. She had a sneaking suspicion that she was the companion Ty had been waiting for all his life. When she really examined her consistent ability to see his good side, she realized she wasn't simply searching for a way to legitimize making love with him. She continually saw good things in him because deep down inside he *was* good. And she decided there must be a reason she saw, as well as a reason why—despite her best efforts—she couldn't help liking him.

But if she told him any of that, he would laugh and try to prove—one more time—that he didn't have a nice side. She had no choice but to bring this to his level. Keep it light. Keep it simple. Keep it about sex or work. Topics he could handle.

"I wouldn't say I'm your perfect companion, but I wouldn't say I'm not, either. Still, somebody's got to break the ice, make you see you're not so bad."

"And you're going to sacrifice yourself."

"Yes."

For several seconds he stared at her, then finally he said, "Are you insane?"

"No, I just have really great parents who have had a passionate romance for almost forty years. I can't imagine anybody not wanting that, but you don't. The only reason I can surmise for why you don't want it is that you don't know it exists. So…"

"I know. I know. You're going to show me."

"Yes."

He closed his eyes and licked his lips, and desire tumbled through Madelyn, stealing her breath and catapulting her thoughts to all the delights that awaited her. This wasn't in any way, shape or form a sacrifice. She genuinely believed that once she showed Ty some real emotion, floodgates of feelings would open for him and he wouldn't be able to keep himself from admitting he felt something for her, too. Because the real bottom line was she liked him. She liked him a lot. She might even be falling in love with him.

He drew a quick breath. "No."

"No?"

"I can't believe, Miss Maddy, that you of all people would use sex to manipulate me." Anger glittered in his black eyes. "Just go to your room and stop playing games."

Madelyn stared at him, her head spinning. Was he right? Had she gotten so confused about her feelings for him that she'd just tried to manipulate him?

That's exactly what happened.

Tears of mortification sprang to her eyes, but the mortification was quickly replaced by embarrassment and humiliation when the real bottom line sunk in. *He'd also turned her down.* No. He hadn't turned her down. He hadn't even taken her offer seriously. All this time she'd thought he wanted her, but he didn't want her. And she'd been too stupid to see it.

She pivoted and bolted from the room.

* * *

Saturday morning, Ty still felt guilty for making Madelyn cry. When he'd seen the tears that sprang to her eyes when he'd told her no, his chest had squeezed as if someone had him in a vice grip. It had taken every ounce of control he had to keep from jumping out of his chair and going after her. But he hadn't because she was a starry-eyed dreamer, and he was a pain-in-the-butt executive. In spite of what she'd said about him deserving a better life than he had, *she* was the one who deserved better than the life she might get stuck with if she didn't stop tempting him.

When he spent far too much of his time wallowing in misery and regret over the fact that he had hurt her, he knew the woman would be the death of him if he didn't fix this. So when she suggested he take the baby to the park for some fresh air, even though he knew she really wanted him to stroll sweet Sabrina through the grassy playground for all the townspeople to see, he agreed.

They meandered through the park twice, and when Madelyn directed him to a bench, he didn't argue. Realizing he wasn't going to get a damned thing done that day unless they resolved this, he sat on the bench and said, "We have to talk."

"There is nothing to talk about."

"Sure, there is. I made you cry."

"From what I've heard, you've made plenty of people cry."

"Yeah, but not over personal things. And that's sort of my point. I don't get personally involved with locals because I am the kind of guy who makes girls like you cry."

"I'm not a girl and I didn't cry."

"I saw the tears."

"Yeah, well, I couldn't help that they sprang up, but by the time I reached my room I felt more sorry for you than for myself. I'm fine."

That didn't make him feel any better. He didn't like that she felt sorry for him, and he knew now more than ever that they had to get on stable footing again. Even if that meant he had to tell her the truth about his life. "Look, I had a fiancée several years ago."

"Somebody with a broom and a cauldron, I'd suspect."

Ty couldn't help laughing at her suspicion that only a witch would go out with him. "At the time I didn't think so, but when she was done with me and my brother, I decided she must have been hiding them in her basement."

Madelyn looked at her nails as if totally disinterested. "Fascinating."

"Come on. At least let me explain why I'm not the kind of guy who has relationships so you know you're not at fault in our disagreement. And we can go back to behaving normally."

She sighed heavily, as if put out, but at least she didn't tell him she didn't care to hear his story.

He drew a quick breath and said, "This woman—Anita—was very beautiful and smart. But she owned a home nursing business that was failing. The problem was she needed to have employees available but she didn't always have jobs for every nurse. Her compromise was to pay them a portion of their salary on the days they were scheduled but she didn't have any work for them. Unfortunately, that meant she was paying people who weren't pulling in an income."

Madelyn shifted on the bench. She might be trying to pretend disinterest, but Ty could tell she was listening.

"So, we bottom lined her unusual employee expense as being a typical start up cost and I bankrolled her business for two years."

Madelyn turned and gaped at him. "You bankrolled her business?"

Hearing the shock and disbelief in her voice, Ty felt his face redden and cursed himself for being so trans-parent around her. "She was my fiancée. Plus, her idea was a good one."

"But she still failed, didn't she?"

"Took my money and ran."

Madelyn studied his face for several seconds then said, "There's more. I can tell."

Ty shrugged, trying to make light of it. "Well, she cheated on me."

"And that embarrassed you enough that you won't get close to anybody else?"

Ty winced. "Yes and no."

"Just spill it, Ty. I'm going to get it out of you eventually."

"Okay, she cheated and Cooper found out. When he told me, though, I didn't believe him and we had a big fight and—"

"And because you didn't believe Cooper, he felt you didn't respect him and he left town."

He sighed, not even slightly confused about why she knew the end of the story. "Seth?"

"He was trying to help me understand the Cooper sit-uation so I could spin it for the press. He ended up help-ing me understand why you behave like such a grouch."

"See, there you go. Even my brother thinks I'm a grouch."

"No. Grouch was my word. Your brother thinks you're a great man. In the same way I can't help seeing goodness underneath your gruff personality, Seth also believes everything you do has an altruistic purpose."

Ty rolled his eyes. "Romantics."

"Seth isn't a romantic."

"He was. But something must have happened. He hasn't told me about it, but it's not our way to pour out our hearts in deep-felt conversations. When he suddenly became quiet and then behaved more maturely at work, I simply recognized that something bad had happened, but it hadn't killed him and he'd learned a valuable lesson. So I let it alone. In fact, I liked the change."

"Because he's becoming like you."

Ty blew his breath out in a disgusted gust. "I'm not Satan. I actually have my good points. But I don't want you going around thinking I'm a nice guy. I want even less for you to go around telling my employees I'm a nice guy."

Madelyn rose from the park bench. "You *are* a nice guy. And I figured out days ago that's why you fight so hard to make people believe you're mean. But this story about your fiancée confirms it. You'd rather strike fear than risk anyone having too much influence over you. You think being grouchy is how you stay in control and successful." She took a quick breath and turned to the sidewalk. "But I think you're into overkill."

With that, she left him alone in the park with Sabrina, and though her parting comment didn't please Ty, he didn't ponder it because he noticed that he wasn't panicked about being alone with Sabrina. He knew he could handle her.

Pride shot through him. He couldn't raise this baby alone, but he most certainly would be a good parent with the help of a nanny to handle the things that didn't require a parent's love.

Realizing what he'd unwittingly admitted, his heart swelled with pride again. He loved this kid. He *loved* Sabrina.

And he owed that to Madelyn.

With the morning sun streaming down on him, his usually tense muscles relaxed, and with one very happy baby sitting in the stroller in front of him, Ty suddenly wondered if Madelyn wasn't right about more than the baby. Maybe Anita had done more damage than he'd thought. Or maybe he'd carried being mean and staying aloof just a bit too far.

Ty behaved oddly when he returned home with Sabrina, but Madelyn simply stayed out of his way. When the first of three potential nannies arrived for her interview later that day, Madelyn went shopping. When the interviews continued on Sunday afternoon, she visited her parents.

Monday morning, Madelyn stuck to her decision to stay out of anything not directly related to Sabrina or PR and left the house for work while Ty chatted—unusually pleasantly—with her parents. But because she'd stopped for a doughnut, she found herself standing next to him at the elevator in the main lobby. She frowned. He wasn't using the private elevator in the side corridor?

She turned to look at him. "Slumming?"

"Experimenting."

What the hell did "experimenting" mean?

Two secretaries entered the lobby and walked to the elevator. "Good morning, Mr. Bryant. Madelyn," they said in unison.

"Good morning, ladies," Ty said and Madelyn gaped at him. *He'd said good morning?*

"Nice day."

"Yeah, it's a beautiful day," Mary McCready agreed.

And Madelyn suddenly saw what he was doing. He was *experimenting* with interacting with his employees. He was *experimenting* with doing the things she'd been trying to get him to do for the past two weeks. He'd *heard* what she'd said on Saturday and he was taking her advice. The realization shocked her so much she let her floor pass and rode with him to the top floor, which held only his office suite.

When she stepped out with him, he said, "Do we have a meeting I don't know about?"

She took a breath. "No."

"Then scram. I have things to do." He walked to Joni's desk and took his messages. He read only one before saying to Joni. "Call that jerk back and tell him we won't do business with his company ever again." He grabbed the message and changed his mind. "No, let *me* call him."

Madelyn turned to the elevator. Tyrant Ty lived. If he was taking her advice by experimenting with her PR suggestions, the changes weren't going to happen overnight, but she wasn't complaining. She *needed* him to mingle with his employees. Taking baby steps into the process was better than not taking any steps at all.

But getting on the elevator, she couldn't stop the voice that whispered to her that advice wasn't the only thing she'd given Ty over the weekend. She'd also given him the cold shoulder. She'd pulled so far away from him emotionally, they could have been living in different houses. His decision to try her advice might be his way of saying that he missed her. God knows she had missed him. Especially when she'd glimpsed how sweet he was with Sabrina in his unguarded moments Saturday evening and Sunday morning. She desperately wanted him to be the nice guy and from his "experiment" it seemed he now wanted that, too.

Her heart leaped and her hope soared. If the nice guy really was coming out, then the time they had to live together until the playground presentation and the *Wall Street Journal* interview would be very different. He might even stop pretending he didn't find her attractive. There was a good possibility he would kiss her again.

When just the thought of having his lips touch hers weakened her knees to the point that she worried about her ability to walk, Madelyn realized the deed was done. She didn't merely like Ty anymore. She loved him.

Or at least she loved the man she knew lived way deep down inside him somewhere. A man who, it appeared from his behavior that morning, was digging his way out. But if the nice guy didn't succeed, Madelyn knew she was in big trouble. The nice guy might be able to love her, but the bossy, pushy tyrant couldn't. And if she didn't handle this correctly, she would get her heart broken.

* * *

Driving home that night, Ty felt restless and irritable. The day had gone remarkably well with him being superconsiderate and polite to his employees. Every meeting ran smoothly. Every discussion came to a satisfactory conclusion. But Ty didn't think the results of his experiment were conclusive. They only proved his employees liked being mollycoddled. They did not prove his business would continue to make money enough to employ an entire town full of people or that Bryant Development would continue to run at the high standards that caused them to win job after job.

The school of hard knocks had taught him that the only way a company stayed on top was by pushing. Pushing, demanding and never backing down had been Ty's edge for so long, he wasn't sure the company would survive if he suddenly became soft. *He* would survive. His employees would thrive—or at least so they thought. But he wasn't sure the company would. And this company was the only thing he and Seth had left of their parents. Changing his business strategy was an enormous risk. Ty wasn't one for taking risks. He thought. He planned. He negotiated. He did not gamble.

Pulling into his driveway, Ty sighed. He was so tired of thinking about this that he wanted two fingers of bourbon, a four-hour sports marathon—any sport would do—and some blessed peace and quiet.

Instead, he walked into the kitchen to find a crying baby and a less-than-civil female who announced there was no dinner and she wasn't cooking.

"Why didn't your mother make dinner?" Ty asked as he rummaged through his cupboards, ostensibly look-

ing for something he could make from among the groceries Madelyn's mother had purchased.

"She had a church thing this afternoon." Madelyn
paused long enough to sigh. "Why don't you just call
Louie's?"

"Because the restaurant doesn't do takeout and I have
to set up some kind of special deal with him."

"Then make some macaroni."

For that Ty turned. "I ate enough macaroni to last a
lifetime after my parents died. I did not become wealthy
to eat like a pauper."

For a few seconds Madelyn stared at him, then in the
cutest, most bubbly way she began to laugh. Ty stared
at her in total confusion. Soon Sabrina stopped crying
and she stared at Madelyn, too.

Ty's eyes narrowed. "Well, that was certainly a cre-
ative way to quiet her."

"I couldn't help it," Madelyn said, using her free
hand to wipe away her tears. "I like macaroni and you
talk about it as if it's poison."

"It's not poison. I've just had my fill."

"Then why don't you take the baby and I'll try to find
something to cook."

Now that Sabrina wasn't crying anymore, that
sounded like a good idea. Ty walked over and slid his
hands around Sabrina's waist to take her from Madelyn,
but as he began to pull Sabrina away, he caught Madelyn's gaze and the strangest thing happened. She smiled
at him and every antsy jumpy nerve, every piece of
stress tightening his muscles, instantly relaxed.

And he finally understood why Madelyn liked him,
because it was the same reason he liked her. When he

was being himself they clicked. Something about her matched with something inside him. She didn't simply challenge him. She also calmed him. And he didn't only push her. He also made her smile. Frequently, he made her out-and-out laugh. He couldn't remember the last person he had been able to make laugh.

They complemented each other. She'd seen it all along. But he was only seeing it now.

He hadn't let anybody get to know him in eight years, but day-to-day dealings had taught Madelyn a lot more about him than he would ever deliberately show anybody. And living with her, he knew some very important things about her, too.

And he liked what he knew. That was why they were drawn to each other. It wasn't sex. It wasn't chemistry. It was a personality connection.

Though it didn't hurt to have the chemistry.

He smiled at her and her face seemed to blossom to life, and he knew everything he had been thinking was true. He liked her. She liked him.

Shifting Sabrina to his right, he bent and kissed Madelyn. As his lips met the softness of hers, his heart seemed to tumble in his chest. He *liked* her. Every molecule in his body sprang to life just being in the same room with her. Kissing her, having his mouth pressed against hers, made him happy. But he wasn't sure he could make the changes she wanted him to make. He wasn't even sure the changes she had already wrestled from him would last. He certainly wasn't sure if what they felt would last forever.

The thought stopped him. Madelyn had never failed him. And he was trying to change for her. But it seemed unfair for them to look at a possible romance as an all-or-nothing circumstance. Particularly since there were hundreds of points of compromise that they were ignoring.

Juggling Sabrina but holding Madelyn's gaze he said, "I have an idea."

"Yes?"

"This thing between us isn't going away."

She shook her head. "I don't think so."

"And you don't believe anything I tell you about me being a nasty man who you should stay away from."

She smiled. "Not even a little bit."

"So I was thinking that maybe what we need is a compromise."

Her brow furrowed in confusion. "What kind of compromise?"

"Well, I like you and you like me. And we're both adults. So maybe that sleeping together idea we've tossed around isn't such a bad one."

She gave him such a horrified look that Ty knew he'd phrased his suggestion all wrong. He tried again. "I'm not just asking you to sleep with me. I'm asking you to compromise. You want me to change. I'm not sure I can. I'm not even sure this relationship will last. But I know for sure it won't even get off the ground unless we meet in the middle."

She smiled, took the step that separated them, and slid her arms around his neck. "Two days ago I would have agreed, but today I don't."

He shifted Sabrina to accommodate Madelyn being close to him. "I assume you have a good reason to back this up."

She stood on her tiptoes and kissed his lips soundly.

Holding Sabrina as he was, he couldn't participate the way he really wanted to and Madelyn pulled back before he could figure out a way to prevent her from breaking their kiss without dropping the baby.

"I know you're going to say I'm wrong, but I think I love you."

His mouth fell open. "After two weeks?"

As if she didn't hear his protest, Madelyn continued, "So I'm not settling for second best. I don't want to sleep with you, I want you to love me."

He gaped at her. He had softened enough to compromise with her and now she was forcing *him* into the all-or-nothing situation? "After two weeks?"

She shrugged. "In some ways, it's very complimentary that you're willing to break a lot of your own personal rules to sleep with me. But if we try things your way and sleep together before you have any real feelings for me, you would be missing out on so much. And I can't let you do it."

His eyes narrowed as he took in everything she said. "Your not sleeping with me is for my own good?"

"Exactly."

"Parts of my anatomy totally disagree with that right now."

"Those parts of your anatomy have been controlling you for too long. This," she said, tapping his chest where his heart would be, "is what I want from you."

With that she turned and began rummaging through the cupboards as if nothing had happened. But Ty knew everything had happened. First, he'd changed his morning routine and begun mingling with his employees. Now, he'd nearly begged a woman to try a relationship with him even though it broke about fifty of his own personal rules, and she'd said no because she wanted his heart.

He almost wished he could give it to her but he knew he couldn't. Not because he needed it for anything else, but because if he gave her his heart, he really would change. He really would lose his edge and his company would go to hell. People would be out of work. His parents' dream would be gone.

And that was the bottom line. He hadn't simply given up on the idea of relationships eight years ago when Anita shafted him. He'd given up his own personal pleasure so that the people of Porter would be employed, his parents' dream would live and he, Seth and Cooper would be respected.

After so many years, he couldn't just throw it all away.

Especially not for a woman.

It seemed insane.

It *was* insane.

And he wouldn't do it.

Chapter Eight

The sun was warm and bright on the morning Ty was to make the presentation of the playground equipment to the day care. Madelyn and Ty hadn't really spoken since their conversation when she told him she wanted his heart, but she had watched him wage a battle of sorts all week. Try as he might, he couldn't go back to being Tyrant Ty. He wanted to. She knew he believed that was how he had become successful. But after his experimental day of being nice to his employees, he simply could not be as cool and remote as he had been. He also couldn't seem to keep his eyes off *her*. More than that, though, she'd seen him reach to touch her several times, then pull back, as if he couldn't prevent his instinct, but refused to succumb to it.

At least not yet. Whether Ty liked it or not, he was changing, and Madelyn decided all she had to do was let nature take its course and soon Ty would be accustomed to this new way of living. And once he got accustomed to his new behaviors, he would realize having her in his life was a big part of that.

But for now there was still a struggle going on. That was why she wasn't surprised when he hired a limousine to take them to the presentation. It was his way of trying to hang on to his former style of doing things. But again, Madelyn wasn't worried. Ty might arrive as the distanced executive determined to maintain the identity he'd built, but once he gave the speech she had written and the townspeople applauded both his comments and his generosity, Tyrant Ty would be a memory.

The chauffeur pulled the limousine onto the back driveway of the two-story frame dwelling on Marigold Street that housed the day care. After a few seconds, the uniformed man opened Ty's door. Ty stepped out and reached in to get Sabrina. The chauffeur assisted Madelyn.

"We won't be more than an hour," Ty told the driver, then faced Madelyn. As he juggled his briefcase and Sabrina, and Madelyn arranged the jacket of her pale peach suit, Seth walked across the grassy backyard.

"Good morning," he said, taking Sabrina from Ty.

"Good morning, Seth," Madelyn said brightly, filled with enthusiasm.

"Good morning, Seth," Ty said, clearly not as upbeat and happy as Madelyn, but she didn't care. She was confident enough for both of them.

"Since the two of you are going to be busy," Seth said, straightening the pink bonnet on Sabrina's head to provide maximum protection from the midmorning sun, "I thought I would take the baby and spend some time getting to know her."

Madelyn watched Sabrina as she cocked her head and studied Seth. The baby had seen Seth only the few times Madelyn had brought her to work. Though he'd held her once, they really didn't "know" each other. Still, Sabrina wasn't afraid of him, simply curious.

"I think it's a good idea for you to spend some time with her," Madelyn agreed.

Ty shook his head. "You mean you're not going to force me to hold her while I make the presentation speech to remind everybody I have a big heart?"

"You do have a big heart," Seth said, but he walked away and Madelyn realized something else she'd been missing up until now. Seth quietly, subtly reminded Ty of his good points as much as she did.

When Seth was gone, Madelyn faced Ty. She and Seth easily saw his goodness, and this morning the residents of Porter would see it, too. Because deep down inside he was a good man.

She straightened his pale-blue tie, then smoothed her fingers down the lapel of his navy blue jacket. "No baby today."

"Wow. You're going to let me loose on the community with no prop."

"You don't need a prop." Hands flattened against his lapels, Madelyn stepped closer. "You're smart," she said, letting herself get closer still. "You're more responsible than any man I've ever met," she added, rising to her tiptoes so their mouths were only a breath apart. "And you look fabulous."

With that compliment, she breached the final space between them and touched her lips to his. She felt his sharp intake of air, but when she pressed in closer, allowing their bodies to touch, she heard the thump of his briefcase falling to the ground. She knew she'd annihilated him the way he had the first time he'd kissed her.

She felt his hands on her back and deepened the kiss. His mouth automatically opened to hers and right there on the sidewalk she took him as high and as far as propriety allowed. Then she stepped back and smiled at the stunned, aroused expression on his face.

"You're also a good man. Not perfect. But good. In fact, I believe that so much, I'm not even going to insist that you give my speech. I want you to go out there and speak from your heart."

His voice was sinfully smoky when he said, "You're not coming with me?"

Madelyn struggled to stay where she was. She wanted to grab his hand, take him home and entice him to fulfill the promise that sizzled between them. But right now it was more important to show him he *didn't* need her.

"Nope. You don't need Sabrina and you don't need me. I want you to see for yourself that these people like you for you." She caught Ty's gaze and held it. "Just as I believe that underneath all your gruffness you're a good man, I also believe that deep down all these people like you. I don't see how anybody could resist you. God knows I sometimes can't. Just be yourself."

With that she walked away.

And openmouthed with pure unadulterated shock, Ty stared at her retreating back. He would have worried that after that kiss he wouldn't be able to think about anything but making love to Madelyn.... Except she'd inspired him. No, she hadn't inspired him. She'd *chal-*

lenged him. She believed he was a good man and she believed these people liked him. If he didn't somehow get them to show it, he would let her down.

And after that kiss he couldn't let her down.

He *wouldn't* let her down.

But he and Madelyn would be doing more than talking after they returned home from this event. Madelyn might think she couldn't sleep with him unless he gave her his heart, but she had enough of his heart for the time being. He might not be giving her the total commitment she wanted or expected, but tonight he wasn't letting her out of her flirting so easily.

Tonight he would prove to her that they were exactly where they were supposed to be for the amount of time they had known each other. He'd compromised enough. It was time for her to do something for him.

With Seth minding Sabrina, and Madelyn making her way to the front of the house to stand with the day-care moms, grandparents and just plain curious Porter residents, Ty walked to the back porch alone. He climbed the steps, but before he reached the screen door, Amanda Jennings opened it.

A short woman, with straight brown hair cut in a line about ear-length and big blue eyes, Amanda resembled a doll. Ty could understand why the kids adored her.

"Good morning, Mr. Bryant."

"Good morning, Amanda. Are we ready?"

"Yes, it's almost ten. I have a table set up on the front porch," she said, leading Ty through a room full of toy boxes and shelves littered with dolls, trucks and board games. "I think this would work best if you said a few words to the people who are gathered, then hand me the truck that symbolizes the gym equipment that will be delivered Monday. I'll thank you for your generosity, then we can cut a piece of the cake that's on the table." She paused and glanced back at Ty. "Since we don't have a ribbon or anything to cut. After that, we'll step out of the way and my staff will finish cutting the cake and serve it."

Ty nodded, but his stomach was tied in knots inside. It was one thing to use the public elevator and say good morning to a few people. It was quite another to stand in front of the spouses, children and parents of his employees and give a donation that could very well be construed as him trying to buy the town's affection before the *Wall Street Journal* reporter arrived on Monday.

Still, after Amanda introduced him, Ty confidently stepped forward and gave the speech Madelyn had written about creating leaders because he believed its message was true. The remarks had seemed like a piece of drivel when he'd first read them. But today he sincerely hoped that somehow or another the care and generosity of a community could inspire a child to become a leader.

When he was done, he turned and handed Amanda the truck that symbolized the equipment he had donated. Overcome with emotion, Amanda unexpectedly hugged him. Ty was too shocked to respond, but eventually he relaxed and returned her hug, genuinely glad that he could do something for his community.

The crowd in the front yard of Amanda's Angels Day Care began to applaud. Slowly at first, but then a momentum grew and soon everyone was cheering.

And for the first time ever, Ty had felt the sense of

community that had been missing from his life. He felt himself connect with the segment of town for whom he had spent his whole life working. He felt his mission in life being accomplished.

And he knew Madelyn was right. If he changed, if he let his real personality out, his employees wouldn't fail him.

But in that moment, Ty also decided she was wrong about something else. He might not love her, but he did need her. She was the force behind all the changing he had done and he appreciated that. It wasn't love, but it was more feeling than he'd had for a woman in almost a decade.

Madelyn wasn't surprised when Ty grabbed her hand as they walked to the limo.

"We did it."

Balancing Sabrina on her right arm, she smiled up at him. "Yes, we did. I told you that deep down these people really liked you. We simply had to give them an opportunity to show you."

Sabrina yelped and patted Madelyn's face as if trying to get a point across. As Madelyn caught the baby's hand to stop her, she saw Ty's expression become confused, then suddenly it brightened, as if he had drawn a conclusion.

"You know what she's trying to tell us?"

Madelyn shook her head.

"That we shouldn't get too cocky. She actually paved the way for this." He took Sabrina from Madelyn and motioned for the chauffeur to come to the car. "If I hadn't needed help with her, you wouldn't have lived with me. If we hadn't had that connection, you wouldn't have gotten me to do half the things I've done. I might have even talked you out of this event."

Madelyn laughed. "I guess, if you look at it that way, she is responsible." She shook her head in wonder. "Fate has been working overtime for us."

Ty's expression shifted. The eyes that had been shining with joy suddenly burned with desire. "Yeah, fate has been doing a lot of things to us lately."

Madelyn's heart rate tripled. Somehow or another, they'd gone from discussing the success of the event to discussing their personal relationship. But she was ready. She'd been expecting a moment of truth after Ty made the presentation. She'd seen him fighting their attraction all week and she knew the approval of the townspeople would help him to accept more of the changes in his life. That was part of why she'd kissed him before she sent him off to make the presentation. She wanted him to be thinking of her when he realized the changes he was making were good.

She stood on her tiptoes and kissed his cheek. "I think this is a discussion better finished in private."

His eyes smoldered. "You're right."

After Ty fastened Sabrina into her car seat, he sat across from Madelyn, but he didn't say anything. They were quiet for the entire drive to his house, but electricity hummed between them. Though Madelyn was confident their upcoming conversation would go well, she forced herself to be pragmatic about what would actually happen.

Ty might be willing to make a concession or two, but he wasn't the kind of guy to fall in love in a few weeks.

All along they'd both admitted they had chemistry and this afternoon he would probably admit that he liked her, but she knew him too well to think he would suddenly be able to say he loved her.

Still, he had changed enough that she knew that some-day he would love her. Even if he couldn't say it, he would probably tell her he had real feelings for her, then their chemistry would take over and they would make love. Be-cause they *both* wanted this, and she wasn't foolish enough to pretend otherwise. And she also wasn't going to be so foolish as to push him, because he'd been pushed enough already. In the past three weeks, he'd learned to care for Sabrina. He'd changed the way he interacted with his employees. He'd given to the community and shown them his real personality in a heartfelt speech. And now he was about to admit to her that he liked her. He couldn't be expected to make the giant leap to love.

Particularly since they had only known each other ex-actly three weeks and a day.

When the driver stopped at Ty's house, Madelyn got out, retrieved Sabrina and took her inside. Because the baby had fallen asleep in the limo, she carried her up-stairs while Ty dismissed the driver.

When she returned to the kitchen, Ty stepped inside the back door. Without a word, she walked over to him. He grabbed her by the waist, hauled her up against him and kissed her so deeply she understood everything he felt for her. He might not be able to say the words, but he couldn't resist her or their chemistry anymore. He was so hungry for her he was desperate. No. *They* were desperate. She was tired of fighting this attraction, too.

His right hand flicked the top button of her suit

jacket. Her fingers went directly for the buttons of his shirt. She considered for a second that the kitchen was the most inappropriate place to do this, then realized that it wasn't. They'd had their best battles here. They'd made concessions here. Worked together here. If she allowed herself to admit it, she would probably also say she'd fallen in love with him here. It could have been that first time he took charge of Sabrina. It could have been that first morning when he ate the burned toast. It could have been the first time he gave her *that* look. The one that melted her bones and caused her to realize he found her more than attractive—he desperately wanted her. Whenever it was, she had fallen deeply, passionately in love with him, and anywhere he wanted to make love was fine with her.

With every button that popped, their kiss grew more heated, until Madelyn felt the pads of his fingers brush the top of her breast at the same time that her fingers met the crisp mat of dark hair on his chest. Arousal flooded through her, a need so sharp and sweet it paralyzed her. His palm covered her breast and she nearly swooned.

Everything felt better, more intense, more powerful because this wasn't just a sex act. At least not for her. She really was making love. And he…might be.

Damn it! In the car she had decided she wasn't going to push him into saying that he loved her, but she knew in her heart that he did. Though it seemed insane to need to hear him say it, she wanted the words.

She pulled away. "Ty…" He stared at her with such heat in his eyes that she fell speechless.

"What?"

Knowing what she had to do, she drew a quick, fortifying breath and simply asked, "Do you love me?"

"Don't even tell me that after teasing me with that kiss at the day care, you've changed your mind."

"I haven't changed my mind." She paused, swallowed, then jumped in with both feet. "But I love you. I *really* love you. And I'm just about positive you love me, too."

He closed his eyes, then opened them again. "We haven't known each other long enough to be in love. But we do have lots of feelings for each other and there's nothing wrong with expressing them physically. In fact, there are lots of times...like right now," he hinted shamelessly, "that expressing feelings physically is very, very good." He caught her arm, pulled her against him and rubbed his cheek against the soft spot in front of her ear. "I will make it very, very good."

Desire rippled through her. She had no doubt that he would make it very, very good. But now that they were this close, she realized something else. Making love for him was the physical expression of what he felt, so if they crossed this barrier without him admitting that he loved her, he would never say it. He wouldn't think he had to. And that wouldn't hurt her as much as it would deprive him. He needed to know he could love and be loved. He needed to hear the words as much as he needed to say them. Everybody did.

She drew a shaky breath. "I realize that if we sleep together, it will be great." She caught his gaze. "But I also suspect that if you don't admit you love me—" she took another drink of air "—you might never say it."

He closed his eyes. "You're killing me."

"Actually, you're killing *me*." She stepped close to

him again, hope welling inside her because he hadn't disagreed. "You love me," she boldly told him. "No matter how much you think you don't, I think you do. All you have to do is say it."

"You think that I love you in a little over three weeks?"

She rubbed her forehead against his chin. "Stranger things have happened."

"Not to me."

Though those three words deflated the hope of the moment, Madelyn didn't feel defeated. "You need more time."

He shook his head. "Madelyn, I'm really not the kind of man to fall head over heels in love." He stepped away from the temptation of her. "And I'm almost getting tired of telling you that. I've laid all my cards on the table. I told you I don't want you unless it's on my terms."

"And I think you've been in denial so long, you don't see what's right in front of you."

"Then you're wrong, and you should button your blouse." With that he walked away. He punched the swinging door and burst through like a man who had no intention of ever coming back.

Madelyn stared after him. Regret and fear washed through her, and she cursed herself for wanting him to love her. She'd done the very thing she'd been telling herself not to do for the past few days when he wasn't speaking to her. She'd lost patience and she'd interfered in his process, and from the tone of his voice she couldn't believe he would even talk to her civilly again, let alone let his guard down enough to love her.

She'd pushed him too far and she'd lost.

Chapter Nine

Ty was so angry he couldn't see straight. With the potent cocktail of fury and sexual heat ricocheting through him, he bounded up the foyer steps and to his bedroom.

He intended only to change into jeans and a T-shirt and retreat to his office for the rest of the afternoon where he would distract himself with work, but decided to take a cold shower. He needed to cool off and not just sexually. He didn't believe anybody could fall in love in three weeks, but for Madelyn to say she had fallen in love with him—a grouch, a guy who had been making her life miserable most of the time they were together—well, that was just preposterous.

To make matters worse, he remembered that this was how Anita had gotten into his life. She'd claimed love at first sight and flattered and teased him until he'd believed her.

He didn't think Madelyn was as devious as Anita

was. But he also wasn't stupid. Smart people learned from their mistakes. And Anita had definitely been a mistake. He'd be a fool to forget the lesson she taught him.

The shower didn't help. Neither did the fact that Sabrina was apparently napping and there was no buffer for him and Madelyn. When Ty ran down the steps, on his way to his office, he saw her pacing in the living room. From the worried expression on her face, it was clear she was upset, but Ty decided she damned well should be. If she was tricking him, her only motive could be to assure she got the job as PR director. But she had to know he would eventually figure that out and when he did, he would deal with her. Most likely, he would fire her. So she damned well better not be teasing him to get the job!

Still, he couldn't shake the notion that Madelyn wasn't that devious. If anything, she was naive. Striding down the hall to his office, he couldn't help drawing the conclusion that if she wasn't making up feelings to manipulate him, then she genuinely believed she loved him.

Ty stopped short as a foreign emotion paralyzed him. What if she really did love him? How the hell would he handle that? He *liked* her. He lusted after her. He lusted after her so much that he couldn't sleep. But he didn't love her. He hadn't known her long enough to love her, but more than that he wasn't sure he *could* love her. He wasn't really sure he could love *anybody*.

Walking into his office he acknowledged that his experiences with love were so distorted that he'd quit trying to see if he was capable of loving someone. Since

Anita, if he courted a woman, it was in the city, and it was with a purpose. To have some fun. He'd never courted a woman to fall in love.

Worse, now that he'd spent so much time refusing to love, he could no longer blame Anita. If he couldn't love, it was because of arrested development. He was a stagnating thirty-five-year-old man who had been hurt and never gotten past it.

Because he didn't want to be hurt again. Because he didn't want his company to suffer. Because he didn't want his community to lose jobs. Because he wanted to keep Bryant Development—his only remaining connection to his parents—strong, vital, alive. For himself…and his brothers.

That was the real bottom line to why he didn't fall in love. There were more reasons not to fall, not to risk, than to give love another shot.

And that's what he had to remind himself every time Madelyn tempted him.

On Monday morning, Madelyn walked down the hall to her office, mentally running through her strategy for the arrival of the *Wall Street Journal* reporter.

Ty's anger with her hadn't changed the fact that he would be giving his interview that morning. Though he had refused to speak to her on Sunday afternoon, not even to let her prep him, she wasn't worried about Ty going one-on-one with a reporter. If she had any concern, it was that their argument on Saturday had caused him to revert back to Tyrant Ty. The reporter wouldn't notice it. He would be gathering facts about the company. But Ty's employees would see the difference.

After the heartfelt playground presentation they wouldn't understand why he'd gone back to being gruff and impersonal. A few people would give him the benefit of the doubt and consider that something might have happened in his personal life that caused him to be preoccupied, but most wouldn't. If the reporter talked to any of Ty's employees to get background for the article, too many of them would say that Ty had given a nice speech and donated some equipment, but he was still the same old Ty. Distant. Removed. Bossy.

Because Madelyn's first responsibility to Ty was as his public relations person, she couldn't dwell on the fact that his refusal to try to love her hurt her. She couldn't give in to the fear that by ignoring what they felt he was hurting himself. She couldn't even let herself feel the guilt of remembering that all of this was her fault because she had foolishly pushed him. Those troubles would still be around tomorrow and she could try to sort through them then. Today she had to focus on finding a way to assure that the right employees spoke with the reporter.

"I'm paying you *thousands* of dollars to find my brother!"

Lost in thought, Madelyn almost didn't hear Seth's angry voice as she walked past his door. But it eventually penetrated her consciousness and she stopped.

Ty hadn't mentioned to Madelyn that he had told Seth to look for their brother Cooper, but she knew Seth had looked for his missing sibling once before and she also knew Ty and Seth had lunch together at least twice a week. It was entirely possible Ty had given Seth instructions to begin looking for Cooper and had simply forgotten to tell her. Still, with the reporter expected in less than an hour, she didn't want Seth giving Ty bad news.

"Don't call me back with another excuse! You find Cooper and you find him now!"

When Madelyn heard the slam of the phone receiver into its cradle, she knocked on Seth's doorframe, then stepped into his office. "Got a minute?"

He drew a quick breath. "I guess you heard that."

"You were a little loud."

"This private investigator is so lazy he infuriates me."

"That's why I came in," Madelyn said, closing the door. "Today would not be a good day to tell Ty your investigator isn't having any luck finding Cooper."

Seth shook his head. "Don't worry, I'm not going to tell Ty. He doesn't even know I'm looking for Cooper."

Madelyn gasped. "Seth!"

Seth sighed in exasperation. "I didn't keep this to myself because I'm sneaky."

"Then why?"

"I didn't consult Ty about looking for Cooper because this search is fruitless and Ty has enough on his mind." Frustration contorted Seth's boyishly handsome features, and Madelyn realized again how different the two Bryant brothers were. Ty had dark hair, dark eyes and dark moods that he seemed to foster to protect himself. Seth was fair-haired with green eyes, and if he currently had dark moods, something had caused them. He was struggling to get beyond it, but couldn't seem to.

Looking tired and worn down by life, Seth fell to his tall-backed leather chair. "What's this world coming to, Madelyn?"

She shrugged and took the seat in front of his desk. "I don't know. But I do know that since I've been here, it's been obvious to me that you have some kind of problem. Something happened to you recently. Why don't you talk to me?"

"Does my brother talk to you about his problems?"

She drew a quick breath. "No. But…"

"No was a good enough answer, Madelyn." He raked his fingers through his hair. "And that's actually the point. Ty gets a problem and he doesn't talk about it. He handles it. I get a problem and I talk about it because I'm looking for help. And do you know why? Because I trust people. Ty never has. Because of that I'm the one who gets hurt. He's the one who doesn't."

Madelyn took a silent breath. Seth had just outlined Ty's entire life philosophy in three or four short sentences. He'd also made Madelyn understand why Ty wouldn't take the last steps to loving her. He couldn't trust. It didn't matter that she'd pushed him Saturday afternoon. The real reason he couldn't fall in love with her was that he couldn't trust. And *that's* what he had been trying to tell her all along.

"I'm not saying that it's good to be a recluse or anything," Seth continued. "I know Ty goes too far. But there are times when it's appropriate to let your private life be private." He caught her gaze. "And I think this is one of them for me. I'm taking Ty's route this time and handling this alone."

Madelyn rose from her seat. "Okay. But when the *Wall Street Journal* interview is completed, do me a favor and tell Ty you're looking for your brother."

He shook his head. "Madelyn, don't get your panties in a bunch over this. My P.I. isn't going to find Cooper. Thank you for being optimistic enough to think I need to share this with Ty, but I don't." He pulled in a shaky breath. "This is my last attempt at finding Cooper. When it fails, I'm done. I simply need something official like a P.I. report that says he's gone, so I can go on to the next step of my life."

"I still think you should tell Ty…." Madelyn prodded hopefully.

He shrugged. "I don't."

"Seth, Ty's going to be mad if you find Cooper or if he just shows up one day when he isn't prepared."

"Come on, Madelyn, Cooper's been gone for eight years. Chances are I'm not going to find him." He caught Madelyn's gaze. "And neither one of us wants my overburdened big brother worrying about nothing. That's why you're also not going to mention this to Ty."

Madelyn gasped. "Oh, no! You might have hired me, but I report directly to Ty. Because of Sabrina, *I live with him.* If you don't tell him, I *have to* tell him."

"Really? You once told me that the PR director was something like the office confessor, the one who needed to be privy to everybody's secrets so she would know how to prevent them from becoming public knowledge. Well, I just told you something I need to be kept confidential. Are you telling me that what you said before isn't true?"

She licked her lips. "This is different."

"Not from where I'm sitting. You came in here as the PR director, wanting to make sure I didn't upset Ty by telling him my P.I. can't find Cooper. Anything I told you I told you as the PR director, expecting confidentiality." He held her gaze with his pale green eyes. "Am I going to get it?"

She licked her lips again. Whether she liked it or not, Seth was right.

"I'll keep your secret. But since you insist I'm speaking as the PR director, I'm also going to give you some advice as the PR director. Tell Ty you're looking for Cooper."

Seth laughed. "Well, if that isn't twisting things around to suit yourself, I don't know what is."

"I'm not twisting things around. I'm giving you the advice you need to hear. If Cooper shows up without warning, Ty will be furious." She turned and began walking to Seth's door. "And he's not going to be angry with Cooper. He'll be furious with *you* for not telling him you were looking for Cooper. Technically, that advice will save your butt…. Which is really why the PR director gets to know everybody's secrets. It's not just my job to keep your reputation intact, it's also my job to tell you how to save your hide." She paused by the door. Before she opened it, she said, "If you're smart, you'll listen."

Ty was immersed in work when the reporter for the *Wall Street Journal* arrived. Madelyn called him from the front desk to let him know she and the reporter were in the lobby and she was bringing him up. Glad the wait was over, Ty put away the files he had been working on and turned off his computer monitor. A few minutes later, there was a knock on his office door.

"Come in," he called, rising from his seat as a young man in his twenties entered with Madelyn. Though the reporter was dressed in a dark suit, white shirt and tie, he didn't look old enough to have graduated from college let alone be the representative of such a prestigious publication as the *Wall Street Journal.*

Madelyn closed the door and said, "Jeff Allen, this is Ty Bryant, Chairman of the Board and CEO for Bryant Development."

Ty rounded his desk to shake the reporter's hand. "How do you do?"

"I'm fine, thank you."

"Have a seat," Madelyn said, motioning for Ty to return to his seat before she directed Jeff to take one of the two chairs in front of Ty's desk. She sat beside Jeff.

"Let's get right to it," Jeff said. "Why am I here? A privately owned company like Bryant Development doesn't usually seek the publicity an article will bring. Why are you now?"

"There are some government contracts we want to bid on," Ty replied, then realized that might have been a question Madelyn wanted to answer. He caught her gaze and she nodded slightly, silently telling him to keep going. He saw the encouragement in her eyes and for a second he wondered why he simply couldn't believe that she loved him, or didn't put some faith in her and take the leap. But this was not the time to think about that and he focused on answering Jeff Allen. "Competition for the projects is stiff. The awards don't go to unknown, untested suppliers and contractors."

As Ty spoke, his confidence grew. He never had a problem talking about his company. It was human contact where he fell short. "We have a great reputation but that won't do us any good if no one knows it."

"And that's your message? That you have a great reputation?"

"No, the message is that we have an experienced, talented staff. That our field people are the best. That we can do any job we bid on."

"Lots of companies can say that," Jeff said, making notations in a small notebook.

"Yeah, but I have reports on successful private-sector projects to back up everything I claim."

Madelyn rose and faced Jeff Allen. "You two don't need me here. But once you're through with Mr. Bryant, Jeff, I'll give you a tour of the office complex."

Before she left the room, however, she gave Ty a quick smile and guilt stabbed at him. All she ever asked of him was that he believe her. He took her advice about Sabrina and he was now a good father. He took her advice about his PR and the townspeople showed him respect. So why didn't he simply let go and trust that she loved him?

Because of Anita. He'd permanently lost Cooper and temporarily lost faith in himself because of trusting someone too quickly. He wouldn't do it again.

More important, though, he suddenly realized that if he didn't do something soon to make Madelyn see he didn't intend to change his mind about loving her, she would get hurt. As of this morning, Madelyn Gentry would be his friend and only his friend. No matter what she said or did he wasn't deviating from that position.

The reporter interviewed Ty until one o'clock, then as PR director Madelyn gave Mr. Allen a tour of the building, introducing him to all of the department heads.

As they walked, she casually tossed out a few employee names by calling out hello, hoping he'd remember those names and choose those people to interview if he went in search of employee testimonials. When the building tour was over, she invited Jeff to lunch, which he accepted, then strolled into Seth's office. Making it appear to be a last-minute decision, she asked Seth to join them.

Ty Bryant's number one cheerleader did exactly as Madelyn hoped he would as they ate at Porter's diner. He talked about Ty. Not intentionally, but how could Seth avoid mentioning Ty's name when he answered questions about his high school years or college, since Ty had been his guardian? Ty had given Seth his first job, taught him how to manage his fortune—actually, it was Ty's business sense that had made Seth rich—and now Ty intended to raise Sabrina.

Every question the reporter asked Seth somehow related back to Ty, and Madelyn sat back and let him talk. Though the article was supposed to be about Bryant Development, most businesspeople ascribed a company's success to its CEO, and having Seth speak of Ty's professional and personal integrity was a perfect way to show the reporter that Bryant Development's domination of its market was no accident.

Lunch lasted until three o'clock. When they returned to the Bryant Building Madelyn said goodbye to Mr. Allen, but knew his interviews weren't over. She hoped his choices for employee interviews would be the people she'd subtly directed him to.

When she glanced out her office window at five o'clock, she saw him approach Orelia Makin, a member of the legal staff who had just returned from Boston after handling a complicated matter—on her own. Ty had been scheduled to go with her, but at the last minute decided to let her go alone. Because Ty had trusted her, she stood taller, walked more efficiently, spoke more eloquently than she had the week before. And Madelyn breathed a sigh of relief. Jeff appeared to be going for the employees she wanted him to talk to.

She wasn't surprised when Ty poked his head into her office at 5:20 p.m., his face wreathed in smiles, his tie loose. "Score another one for the home team."

Madelyn laughed. "I guess that means you're satisfied with the way your interview went?"

"Absolutely."

Madelyn had never before seen Ty look so relaxed or so pleased and she realized he wasn't being Tyrant Ty. Whatever damage she had done on Saturday by pushing him had been undone by the success of his interview. Seeing how quickly he had rebounded, she also knew that, though he would suffer setbacks, he would never permanently return to being the reclusive, distant man he had been. She really had done her job as PR person for Bryant Development. The only thing he hadn't been able to do in the past three weeks was fall in love with her.

That broke her heart. Not only because it hurt her, but also because she knew they were good together. She knew she made him happy. She knew she could love him forever, but she finally understood why he didn't even want to try. He genuinely believed he could not trust her, and love required trust. That hurt her, but what Ty didn't understand was that in the long run he would hurt himself more.

Still, she smiled when she said, "Then we're ready to go home."

"I'm going to call Louie's for dinner."

"Great," she said, following him out to the hall and into a waiting elevator. When he pressed the button for the first floor, she said, "Don't you want to go back to your office and get your briefcase?"

"I'm not working tonight."

Taken aback, Madelyn stared at him. "What are you going to do?"

"Well, I have to make some calls to set up final interviews for my two nanny choices. Then I thought I'd relax a bit."

"Doing what?" Madelyn asked as the elevator door closed.

He shrugged. "It's been years since I watched anything but football or basketball on TV. Maybe I'll check that out."

They stood in silence, Ty with his jacket open, his tie loose and his hands shoved comfortably in his trouser pockets and Madelyn clutching the handles of her briefcase and her purse, knowing her mouth was probably slightly open in shock. Deciding to spend an evening watching television was so uncharacteristic of Ty that she was speechless. More than that, however, the unexpected choice pointed to something neither one of them had anticipated. They still didn't know how far his changes would take him. Though he seemed so positive he would never love anybody, he really couldn't say that for sure. Given enough time, it appeared he could change his behavior about almost anything.

She wondered if her real course of action shouldn't be to simply figure out a way to stay around in his life until he realized he had feelings for her. Real feelings. Feelings that could keep them together forever.

Technically she already had the perfect way to stay in his life. All she had to do was get the job as his PR director and she'd be right under his nose for as long as she needed to be.

Chapter Ten

When they arrived at Ty's house, he said, "I have Louie's number in the den."

Madelyn said, "Okay," but didn't follow him. Instead, carrying Sabrina, she raced upstairs, intending to change into…

She paused in front of the closet she was using in Ty's spare bedroom. Change into what?

Juggling Sabrina on her hip, she sighed. "What does a woman wear to get a man to give her a job without forgetting she's a woman?"

Sabrina laughed.

Madelyn frowned, looking again at the things in her closet. If she wanted to seduce Ty, she could make anything sexy. But what did a woman wear to make a man interested in her both as an employee and a woman?

Setting Sabrina on the bed, Madelyn caught her reflection in the mirror. She wore a simple emerald-green suit with an ecru blouse beneath and a strand of pearls. Her hair was pulled into a professional-looking bun. After a few seconds of thought, she took off her suit jacket and freed the top two buttons of her rather sedate blouse, leaving her strand of pearls on her neck. There. Sort of sexy but not blatant. Also still businesslike enough to remind Ty she was in his life because she worked for him.

She glanced at her hair. The professional bun. Maybe a tad too professional?

The blouse and skirt were enough to remind him that she worked, had a brain and should get the job as PR director for Bryant Development because she'd done exactly what they'd hired her to do. The two open buttons of her blouse proved she was relaxed, but relaxed wasn't feminine. And she wanted to make sure Ty saw she could fill both the professional and personal spots in his life.

She loosened her bun and let her hair fall clumsily, sexily to her shoulders. Yeah. That was it. The loose, sexy hair. It didn't look like something she'd done on purpose, only appeared as if she'd taken out her bun. But in a world of business suits, pearls and opened buttons, the sexy red hair was her trump card.

After changing Sabrina, Madelyn took her to the kitchen and fed her cereal. Then she carried the baby into the dining room where two places were set at the shiny oak table, Ty's at the head and hers beside it. She slid Sabrina into her high chair as Ty entered the room, holding the takeout containers.

"Hey. Food just got here," he said, as if making an announcement to a casual friend, but his words stopped when he looked at her hair. She watched his gaze fall to the two open buttons of her blouse, but he didn't mention either her hair or the relaxed way she was dressed. He set the cartons of food on the table then pulled out her chair.

She smiled politely. "Thanks." As she sat, she caught a whiff of salmon and her stomach growled. "Oh, wow. That smells great."

"I love salmon. I hope that's okay with you." He took his seat at the head of the table and motioned for her to help herself to the takeout.

"Yeah. I love it, too."

She served herself from the takeout containers. Then Ty dug in. He didn't say another word, simply began to eat, and Madelyn's nerves tightened. She should have forgotten about getting him to notice her as a woman tonight and focused on getting him to give her the job. "So, tell me more about the interview."

"It went beautifully. You were right. I was myself and everything worked out."

Madelyn held back a sigh of relief. Not only did the interview go well, but also he gave her the credit for steering him in the right direction.

"I think the follow-up questions Jeff had for employees went well, too. I can casually walk around the building tomorrow…you know, ask about the interview and see if the people he spoke with will tell me what they said."

"Good. I'd like to know."

"Okay. No problem."

Silence stretched between them again as they ate. Madelyn wondered if in all the stress of hiring nannies, and giving the playground presentation and the interview, Ty hadn't forgotten about the PR job. If he had, she wasn't going to remind him. Eventually, Seth would approach him about it and she didn't want to look foolish or overeager by bringing it up when her work was supposed to speak for her. So she changed the subject. "Anything else interesting happen today?"

Ty hesitated, as if considering his answer, then said, "I had an odd conversation with Seth."

Oh, no! Maybe they did talk about her getting the PR job! And maybe he was behaving oddly because the result wasn't good! After all, her getting the job wasn't the only issue. Ty had never really been sure he wanted a PR department.

"He was talking like a man who is leaving."

Because that wasn't what she was expecting to hear, Madelyn's breath whooshed out. "Leaving?"

"Yeah." Ty set his fork down on his place mat and gave Madelyn his full attention. "It was the strangest conversation. He said something about being restless, wanting more…feeling something is missing and that he wants to look for it."

Madelyn swallowed. This was just peachy. She'd led Ty directly to the one topic she had to avoid because she had promised Seth confidentiality. "Maybe he's just going on vacation?"

"His comments didn't sound like vacation comments. He was talking like a guy who was job hunting."

"Because he said he was looking for something that's missing?"

Ty shrugged. "What else could be missing? He's got money. He has a position. Women fall all over him. The only thing 'missing' in his life is the challenge of seeing if he could make it on his own."

Not knowing what else to say, Madelyn said, "Oh."

Ty sighed. "What if he takes a job in another state then doesn't come back, like Cooper?"

Hoping she could steer a conversation about Cooper into a conversation about anything other than Seth looking for Cooper, Madelyn said, "The way I heard the story, Cooper didn't come back because he was angry."

"And he stays away because he's happy."

The way Ty phrased that made Madelyn think he knew where Cooper was, and if that was the case she really had to get these two brothers talking. She might not be able to tell Ty that Seth was looking for Cooper, but she could sure as heck get them in the same room and tell Seth to start talking. "You *know* Cooper's happy?"

"Reasonably happy." Ty peered at her. "You don't think I would let my brother go off on his own without at least checking to be sure he wasn't starving in some flophouse?"

No. She knew better than that. That was part of the reason she loved him. He was responsible.

"But I won't contact him. I tried about five years ago. I offered him one-third of our company. He refused it. He had an attorney call me and threaten to go after a restraining order if I didn't stay out of Cooper's life." Ty closed his eyes but quickly opened them again. "He hates me, Maddy."

"Oh, Ty! Don't say that. You don't deserve that."

"He thinks I do." Ty rose from his seat and began to pace. "Hell, most days I think I do. I didn't believe him at a point in time when he was most defenseless."

"You made a mistake."

"Yes, I did. That's why I don't want to make a mistake with Seth. I don't want him to leave our company. I want him to stay. Hell, if he wants to be challenged, I'll give him a challenge." Uncharacteristically vulnerable, he turned to Madelyn. "But how can I give him a challenge if he only talks in vague terms and won't come right out and say what he wants?"

Madelyn couldn't answer. Though she understood the question and even knew Seth's rationale, something else unexpectedly occurred to her. Ty considered her a friend, someone he could confide in, or he wouldn't be talking about Seth and Cooper the easy way he was. But, confusingly, he was being very careful not to make too much eye contact.

"And I'm going to lose him, Madelyn. He's going to run out into the world to try to find himself and he's not going to come back."

Madelyn continued to study him, as something else struck her. He wasn't simply avoiding eye contact. With the exception of his two-second glance at her hair and blouse, he'd hardly looked at her at all.

She took a breath and tried not to think about the things she was noticing and focus on the discussion. "Okay, first of all. you don't know that. Second, he hasn't gone. He may not go. Why not cross all those bridges when you come to them?"

"You're right." He sat again. "I'm borrowing trouble. Forget I said anything."

"No, I don't want to forget you said anything. I'm glad you can talk to me."

He glanced at her and smiled. "I'm glad to be able to talk to you, too."

There wasn't a drop of real warmth or intimacy in Ty's smile, and Madelyn suddenly understood what was going on. He'd relegated her to the role of friend. He knew she wasn't going to be leaving his life—not if he gave her the PR job. So, to make it logical that he confided in her, took her advice and spent time with her, he called her his friend and suddenly everything they felt for each other was reduced to a simple, acceptable role.

"Ty," she began, stretching his name out, stalling, not quite sure how to approach the subject. Finally she knew the direct route would be best. "Did you make the decision today that we were only going to be friends?"

"Madelyn, I don't have many friends." Saying that, he caught her gaze, and Madelyn knew he wanted her to really understand what he was about to say. "This is as good as you're going to get from me."

"Because you're so sure you can't trust enough to fall in love?"

"Because I don't think we're right for each other." He drew an exasperated breath. "Madelyn, I'm ten years older than you are. I'm established. You're just starting out. Our lives are in two different places."

Sabrina banged on her tray and Ty turned to pick up the rattle she had dropped and handed it back to her. "And if that's not enough to make you see we're totally unsuited, I come with a ready-made family. I have a baby. I also have two brothers whose lives are a mess. You don't want me."

"Yes, I do," she argued, feeling she had to make this last-ditch appeal. "You're sexy. You're handsome. You're strong. You're smart…and, yes, you're responsible. Those are all reasons to love you."

He shook his head. "Then maybe what I'm saying is that you don't fit into *my* life except as a friend."

"No, what you're really saying is that you can't take the risk. So it's easier to tell me we're unsuited, but you'd like to be my friend. That way you don't have to try to have a relationship or hurt me with a complete rejection that will cause me to walk out of your life."

"Did you ever stop to think that I'm trying to protect *you?* I have a child! I run a multimillion-dollar business, and if that isn't enough to keep me busy, toss in two brothers whose lives are always in some kind of turmoil."

"Your brothers are adults who can take care of their own problems. If you're in their business, you're meddling. And in case you haven't noticed, I love Sabrina, too. She's been part of the package for me all along."

"Not really. You might have helped with her, but responsibility for her has always been mine. Up to now, you've been playing house."

Madelyn gaped at him. "Playing house?" His comment stunned her so much she was forced to wonder if they weren't unsuited. Anybody who had the audacity to accuse her of playing house hadn't been paying one whit of attention to what was going on. And maybe *that* was the problem. Maybe hoping for anything real between them was pointless because he didn't see her actual place in his life. And maybe it was time for her to accept that.

She rose. "You know what? I'm tired of arguing. I think we would be very good for each other. You don't. And there's no middle ground. I'm going home to pack for Atlanta."

He tossed his napkin to the table and rose, too.

"Madelyn," he said through a long-suffering sigh, "you don't want to go back to Atlanta when there's a good job here in Porter for you."

"No, thanks. I refuse to be the town old maid, pining after a guy who'll be perfectly happy to be my friend, but who'll never see me as anything else."

"The town old maid?"

"If I accept your job, you would keep me on your staff, as your trusted friend, and I would never break away. I would always have the stupid hope that some day you would see it's not a mistake to love me. But you never will, will you? I'll be another Cooper. Somebody you can't completely control, but somebody you keep on a short leash."

"That's ridiculous."

"Not really. But you have a right to your opinion just like I have a right to mine. I have to handle my life the way I see best for me."

"What about your parents? I thought you wanted to live close to them?"

Madelyn noticed that in all the arguments he made to get her to stay, he never once said the company needed her, or the employees would miss her, and especially not that *he* would miss her. He argued everything but the things that might get her to reconsider or at least weaken. Almost as if he wanted her to be clear that if she stayed, she stayed for her reasons…not for any reason that would make him indebted to her.

"I would like to live in Porter in case my dad has another heart attack. I would also like to live here so my parents could enjoy my children—if I ever have any—since all their other grandchildren live in different states.

But I'm not going to be another person you fit into your
life the way you want me to fit. No matter where you
put me, I'll still love you. Every day I'll probably love
you a little bit more. But every day as you get accustomed to seeing me as only a co-worker, you'll forget
you might have had even the tiniest bit of feeling for me
once upon a time."

He didn't even hesitate. "Madelyn, I'm doing this for
your own good."

"Then you're nuts."

Madelyn walked out of the dining room with her
head high, but before she turned to go, Ty could see in
her eyes that her heart was broken. For the first time in
his life he wished that he could love someone, that his
life wasn't so crazy and difficult, but he was who he was
and he had the life he had.

And he also knew she deserved better than him.

Chapter Eleven

When Madelyn left his house, Ty called Fran Baker, one of the two candidates he had chosen for the nanny position, and told her she had the job. Then he spent a nearly sleepless night, worried about Seth, worried about Madelyn, wondering why the hell so many people were dreamers.

Fran arrived the next morning at ten o'clock as they had agreed, and he brought Sabrina into the den and put her in her walker with some toys while they finalized her employment agreement.

He worked from home the rest of that week, as Fran and Sabrina got adjusted to each other, and he realized Madelyn had taught him to think of things like that. He told himself to stop relating everything to her, but everything in the house reminded him of her. When Fran laughed at something Sabrina did, he heard Madelyn. When he burned his morning toast, he remembered

Madelyn telling him any burned toast was his. When he bathed Sabrina to get her ready for bed, he realized Madelyn taught him the football hold.

She taught him everything he knew about babies. And PR. But she hadn't taught him anything else because when it came to life, she was naive. She might know how to diaper a baby and get a reporter to see the good rather than the bad, but she didn't yet realize that life was complicated. It wasn't easy. It wasn't supposed to be fun. At least not for people like him.

And as for her saying he kept Cooper on a short leash... Well, that just made him mad. He couldn't believe she had gall enough to insinuate that he didn't have the right to keep track of his brother, and was glad—damned glad—she had gone. Or was going. He hadn't been out of the house to officially hear that she'd actually left town. But she would. There really wasn't enough work for a public relations person in Porter, and if she wanted a job, she would have to move to a big city. And he was not taking the blame. He had offered her the job she wanted. *She* refused it.

Ty spent so much time thinking about Madelyn, he was eager to get back to work the following Monday. His first order of business was straightening out Seth. He silenced the little voice that reminded him Madelyn and her interfering in his adult brothers' lives was meddling, because it wasn't. His brother was one-third owner of the most successful developer in his state. Only a fool would throw that away. Ty would not let another of his brothers live close to the poverty line, just because he was stubborn.

Ty had Joni call Seth into his office, and when Seth arrived he cut right to the chase. "What's going on with you?"

Seth laughed and fell to a seat in front of Ty's desk. "What's going on with you is a better question. You haven't been here in a week!"

"I was home getting Sabrina adjusted to her new nanny."

"That confirms one rumor I heard at the diner. But I heard another, more interesting rumor. I attempted to confirm it, but Madelyn wouldn't take my calls when I tried to reach her at her parents' house."

"If the rumor you heard is that Madelyn refused to work for us, then you're batting two for two."

Seth stared at him. "What did you do?"

Righteous indignation flooded Ty. "What do you mean what did *I* do?" This was why he meddled—if he really meddled. He wasn't accepting that accusation just yet. He got the blame for everything that went wrong anyway. At least when he got involved, one of two things happened. Things either worked out or he deserved the responsibility for the failure. "How do you know she simply didn't decide this job wasn't right for her?"

"Because I know Madelyn."

"Well, good for you, but I offered her the job and she refused it. So, it's time to move on. I want to know what's going on with you. Are you thinking of leaving?"

Before Seth could answer, the intercom on Ty's desk buzzed and Joni's voice came through the speaker. "Ty, there's an attorney on line one."

"Tell him I'm busy."

"I already did. He said if you didn't take his call, there would be a court order on your desk before noon."

"A court order? For what?"

"He didn't say."

"Damn it!" Ty grabbed the receiver and punched the button for line one. "What?"

"Mr. Bryant, this is Gil Montrose. I represent your brother Cooper. He's asked me to remind you that you promised not to interfere in his life."

"I'm not interfering in his life!" This one he knew with absolute certainty. He might keep track of Cooper's whereabouts, but he hadn't *done anything*. He simply watched sadly as his brother struggled.

"Then perhaps you would like to explain why there's a private investigator asking about him."

Because Ty's source of information about Cooper was not a private investigator, he calmly said, "I have no idea."

"Mr. Bryant, it will only take me a few phone calls to find out who hired him, so stop pretending…"

"No! You stop! I made a promise to my brother five years ago that I would not interfere in his life and I not only do not interfere in his life, I also didn't send an investigator to check on him."

With that Ty slammed down the phone, and when he looked at his brother, Seth was cringing.

"You're the one looking for Cooper, aren't you?"

"Yes. But it sounds like you already know where he is. Like you've always known."

At the accusing tone of Seth's voice, Ty groaned. "Damn it, Seth, what was I supposed to do? I had to make sure he was okay, but he doesn't want us in his life. I couldn't tell you where he was."

"Were you afraid I'd just go and visit him someday?"

"Yes. He doesn't want us visiting him and I felt that if you knew where he was you might some day get in a mood and go to Texas."

"Well, thank you very much for trusting me and treating me like an adult."

Ty jumped out of his seat to pace. "Don't you start, too!"

"What do you mean, don't start, too?" Seth asked, his voice sounding angry. "Who else have you been talking with about Cooper?"

"I talked with Madelyn!" And now he could hardly remember why. Confiding in her came so naturally that he'd told her way too many of his secrets and now he didn't remember how Cooper had come into conversation to defend himself to Seth.

Seth studied Ty for a second. "You told Madelyn about Cooper?"

Ty sighed. "Didn't I just say that?"

"You told her, but you wouldn't tell me?"

Ty returned to his seat. "I'm not going over this again."

Seth stared at him. "You really don't get it, do you?"

"What? I have no idea what you're talking about."

"You have two brothers who are adults. Yet, you haven't really let me out of your sight much in the past fifteen years and somehow or another you're monitoring Cooper."

"All right. When you put it like that it sounds as if I'm some kind of overbearing big brother, and it's not like that," Ty said, totally aggravated now. "But you know what? It doesn't matter if I was overbearing or not. I'm done. If you two want to be responsible for yourselves, I will let you."

Seth grinned. "Well, thanks."

Furious, Ty returned to his chair. He absolutely was not saying you're welcome. Seth made him feel like an idiot for caring for his own brothers, but he wasn't an idiot. He was responsible. In a week or a month, Seth would see...

What? Ty unexpectedly wondered. Seth was thirty. Nothing was going to happen to him if Ty backed off.

He picked up his pen, then tossed it down again. "All right. Look, I get it. I've been a little too present in your life."

"And Cooper's?"

He shook his head. "No. I really have stayed out of Cooper's life. I just sort of keep tabs."

"Well, stop that, too."

"Seth, I offered him one-third of our company and he threw it back in my face. I've been holding his share of the profits in an account that's his to use. He said he doesn't want it, but he's just barely living above the poverty line. He *needs* it."

"He was really mad when he left."

Ty nodded. "And apparently he's still mad."

"So maybe we should figure out a way to make him unmad. There's got to be a way we can get him to take the money." Seth paused and drew a quick breath. "Especially if he needs it."

"He does, but in the past five years I haven't thought

of a way to get him to accept an apology, let alone take his money." Ty paused. He hadn't had any luck with Cooper, but Seth had always had a closer relationship with their middle brother. He quietly added, "Maybe you should give it a shot."

Seth grinned. "Maybe I should." He rose from his seat.

"Okay, but no more private investigators," Ty said. "Cooper lives in Texas. He bought a ranch with a friend, but it's mortgaged to the hilt. He drives a truck to pay the mortgage. That's about all I know and about all you get to work with to figure out how we can get him to take his share of the company."

"That's good enough!" Seth said, then left the office.

And silence echoed around Ty. It didn't feel weird to give Seth the assignment of figuring out a way to get Cooper to take his share of the company profits. It felt right. It also felt right to take a step back from Seth's life. After all, Seth was thirty and Ty had another Bryant to raise in Sabrina. It wasn't like he needed to be interfering in his adult brothers' lives to keep himself entertained. He wouldn't be bored.

He leaned back in his seat and closed his eyes. Actually, with all the honesty that had floated around his office in the past few minutes, he felt compelled to admit, if only to himself, that he was bored. It was why he'd sent Orelia Makin to Boston. Negotiating had lost its appeal. Even building had lost its appeal. He didn't intend to stop. But he just didn't get the big kick out of running the company that he had in the past years.

And that was why he decided he couldn't stay in the office that morning. With his brothers' lives out from under his care, Sabrina very squarely in his care, and Seth figuring out a way to get the situation with Cooper straightened out, his life was suddenly totally different from what it had been only the month before. It wasn't exactly empty, but it wasn't in sync, either.

He knew he needed to think this through. He left the Bryant Building, got into his SUV and simply started driving. He didn't know where he would go or what he would do, but after only a few blocks he understood what he was feeling. He had time on his hands and mental energy. And the thing that kept popping into his head was that he now had time for everything Madelyn wanted.

He gripped the steering wheel. Even talking to Madelyn would open the doors to things he wasn't sure he could handle. She didn't just want to spend time with him. She wanted him to love her. And all along he'd told her he didn't think he could love anybody. Talking with Seth, giving him the burden of getting Cooper to accept his share of their profits, hadn't changed that. A relationship with somebody like Anita could ruin a man for life. How fair would it be to drag Madelyn into a relationship when he couldn't promise he wouldn't hurt her?

Still, he found himself driving on her parents' street, and to his horror he watched her pulling out of the driveway. She turned her little blue car in the opposite direction and didn't see him, but Ty saw that the back of her car was packed with her possessions.

She was leaving.

He let her get far enough ahead of him that she

wouldn't see he was behind her, and followed her. Twice, he nearly turned off onto a side street to get away from her because he had no clue what he intended to say or do if she realized he was following her and confronted him. But though he kept going slower, staying as far behind as he could, he couldn't turn away. Eventually she pulled into the convenience store for gas. By the time Ty reached the store, she was standing by the pumps, shoving her credit card into the little slot.

Without allowing himself to think through what he would say or even what he wanted, he swerved his SUV into a parking space in front of the store, jumped out and walked over to her.

"Hey."

Madelyn pushed a wayward strand of hair out of her face. "What are you doing here? Shouldn't you be working?"

"I just had a talk with Seth."

She grimaced. "Oh, yeah? How did it go?"

"He asked me to stop meddling in his life."

She grimaced again. "Ouch."

"Yeah, but a funny thing happened as we were talking. Things I thought were okay to do for my brothers I suddenly realized were overbearing."

Madelyn smiled smugly. "Really?"

"Don't gloat. Once I admitted Seth was right and that I kind of did take on all the responsibility for everything myself, I told him where Cooper was. I told him that the real deal with our middle brother was that he was broke and we had to figure out a way to get him to accept his share of the profits of Bryant Development. And I gave Seth the job."

"You gave him the job of fixing the situation with your brother?"

"Yeah, pretty freaky, isn't it?"

Madelyn laughed. "Yeah!"

Ty nodded at her packed car. "Where are you going?"

"Atlanta."

"You haven't changed your mind?"

Though Ty thought she would laugh, she looked away, and he saw a sheen of tears come to her eyes. "No."

His chest tightened. It was his moment of truth. Though he didn't think he was ready for everything she wanted, he couldn't let her leave, either. "Why don't you take the PR position?"

She shook her head. "I don't think so."

"Look, you did a great job with the day-care presentation and the reporter. Let's just start by officially giving you the position as director of PR—" he caught her gaze "—and see what happens with everything else."

She shook her head again. "Thanks, but no thanks."

Frustration ricocheted through him. They were back to where they always were. "Please don't tell me you want me to love you."

"I want you to love me." She pulled the hose from her gas tank and replaced it in the pump. "You do, you know."

He stared at her, completely amazed she had ever had the audacity to call *him* stubborn.

"But you don't want to say it because you're afraid of taking a risk." She pulled a paper towel from the container beside the windshield washer fluid and began wiping the grime from the gas pump off her palms. "But that means you put me in a situation where *I* have to risk. I've already explained that taking that job when you don't love me puts me in an awkward position. Because I love you, if I come to work for you, I will look like a pathetic loser pining after a man who can't love her. The only way this works, the only way I can stay—" she caught his gaze "—is if you love me."

He swallowed. He got what she was saying. If he didn't say the words she needed to hear to stay in town, then she risked looking like a fool if he could never say them. At the same time he couldn't lie.

And he knew the very second she figured that out. The tiny light that had been in her eyes suddenly died. Her lips parted slightly and her tongue darted out to moisten them, as if she were giving herself something physical to do so she wouldn't completely dissolve with disappointment.

"Well, I guess that settles that," she said, and turned toward her car door.

Regret tumbled through Ty. Not just that she was leaving, but that she was leaving so hurt. She'd totally changed his life for the better, but in the process he had hurt her.

As she pulled the lever that opened her car door, Ty remembered their time together frame by frame. And every frame included her laughing, her smiling, her teasing. Her pushing him, challenging him, refusing to be bullied by him. She was nothing but emotion. And in a life that had been totally devoid of emotion for at least eight years, she was like water on cracked, dry land. Her laughter had been the first in his life for years. He suddenly didn't know how he could live without that. Minutes, hours, days, weeks, months, years loomed before him empty and void.

As she prepared to step inside her car, he saw himself quietly grow old. He saw Seth fall in love and start a family. He even saw Sabrina grow up and move away from him. And he saw himself alone and lonely because, without the woman stepping into the car, he lived in a dry, arid desert. And he didn't want to live in the desert anymore. He wanted her warmth, her laughter, even her confrontations.

And if that wasn't love, Ty was willing to take the risk that it was.

"I love you."

He watched Madelyn pause halfway to the seat of her car, then quickly shift to face him, eyes wide with disbelief. But that wasn't nearly as satisfying to Ty as the sensation that burst in his chest.

He *did* love her.

"I do love you," he said, disbelief and hope mingled in his voice. "My, God! I love you!"

Madelyn fell into his arms. "Why do you sound so surprised?"

He looked down at her upturned face. Her full lips had tipped up into a smile. Happy tears had filled her eyes. Her pretty hair glistened in the sun. He knew he wasn't surprised that he would want this woman in his life. What surprised him was that it was so easy.

He swallowed. "It's so much easier than I thought it would be." As a weight lifted from his shoulders, hope and joy filled him. He never wanted to lose this feeling, this woman. "Stay."

She pulled back and looked at him.

Before she could protest, challenge him or make the suggestion, he said, "Marry me." For once he wanted a decision about their lives to be his idea, not the end result of her prodding.

Her mouth fell open. "Are you sure?"

"I have never been more sure," he said, then he kissed her. His mouth met the softness of her lips and he finally realized that the sensation he felt every time he kissed her was rightness, perfection, partnership. This was the woman who was supposed to be in his life. This was the woman he *loved*. He kissed her lips, her cheeks, her eyes, then he brought his mouth to her lips again where he deepened the kiss, letting his tongue explore her mouth while his hands freely roamed along her body. She was his. He finally understood that.

A car pulled up to the pump beside them. Ty continued to kiss Madelyn. Like a starving man at a banquet, he couldn't get enough.

A car door slammed. "Hey, buddy, get a room."

Ty pulled away and faced the guy. Jim Ronan from Bryant Development's Estimating Department. "Hey, Ronan. Wanna have a job on Monday?"

"Mr. Bryant!"

"It's Ty. And just pump your gas." He faced Madelyn again. "So, do you want to go to your parents' house and tell them you're staying…" He lowered his voice.

"Or my house. We'll send the new nanny and Sabrina on a mission, and make love."

She rose to her tiptoes and kissed him. "Your house. There'll be plenty of time to settle things with my family."

"Family," Ty said, suddenly realizing something else. "You do understand that Seth trying to get Cooper to take his share of the profits may end up bringing Cooper back into our lives."

"Actually, I think that's what you guys need to have happen."

He looked at her, and realized that she was right. It wasn't enough to get Cooper to take the money. They had to get their brother back in their lives. "You're right." He pulled her to him again. "We're gonna have a lot of fun."

"You missed a lot of fun." She kissed him again. "And I'm just the person to make it up to you."

* * * * *

Coming this July from NEXT™

When things don't work out the first time—
there's always Plan B....

THERE'S ALWAYS PLAN B by Susan Mallery

A warm, witty novel from *USA TODAY* bestselling author Susan Mallery and Harlequin NEXT

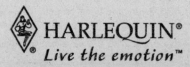

SILHOUETTE *Romance* ®

COMING NEXT MONTH

#1778 THE TEXAN'S RELUCTANT BRIDE—
Judy Christenberry
Lone Star Brides
Thomasina Tyler had no interest in settling down. But the marriage-minded Peter Scholfield had other ideas. For this cautious beauty had captured his interest, and the mouthwateringly handsome executive always got what he wanted!

#1779 FAMILIAR ADVERSARIES—Patricia Thayer
Love at the Goodtime Café
She was the rich girl, he was the rancher's son. And now that she was back in town, the chemistry between Mariah Easton and high school sweetheart Shane Hunter was stronger than ever. But a long-standing family feud would force Mariah to choose between her family and the man of her dreams....

#1780 FLIRTING WITH FIREWORKS—Teresa Carpenter
Blossom County Fair
Mayor Jason Strong was devoted to keeping order in his small town. Only an exotic stranger with an impish glint in her eye was disturbing the serenity of his quiet community. If the handsome widower and single father didn't watch out, the sparks flying between him and the lovely Cherry Cooper might make his peaceful life explode!

#1781 THE MARINE'S KISS—Shirley Jump
Nate Dole had plenty of experience on the battlefield, but that didn't prepare him for Jenny Wright's third-grade classroom! The feisty children had the once-hardened marine thinking twice about the merits of civilian life...especially if it included stolen moments with their alluring teacher.

SRCNM0705